The White Girl

Sa'id Salaam

Published by Black Ink Publications, 2020.

THE WHITE GIRL

First edition. April 12, 2020.

Written by Sa'id Salaam.

Chapter 1

"Oh my God! Look at her eyes!" Mary, the proud new mother gushed, as her newborn was placed into her arms.

"Wow! Crystal Blue, just like the water in Belize," Bob said reminiscing on the beautiful vacation spot the new addition to the Atkins family was most likely conceived.

"That's what we will call her!" Mary exclaimed. "Crystal, Crystal Blue Atkins."

"Hello Crystal. I'm your dad," Bob sang sweetly, unaware of the fact that he just may have been otherwise.

Mary and Bob met at a party on the campus of Georgia University during their sophomore year. It was a chance meeting when Bob decided to take his first drink.

Bob came from a working class home in suburban Ohio. Tall, handsome, and intelligently nerdy, he was the first of his clan to attend college. He studied hard in his pre-law major and had a great future ahead of Mary. Mary was the lovely daughter of a prominent Atlanta surgeon and his socialite wife. She attended Georgia University at her father's insistence, and for fear of getting cut off if she didn't.

She partied hard at the school, which was known for its hard partiers, and was sexually liberated. Most weekends were spent drinking, snorting, smoking, popping pills and fucking. She was by some accounts a "free whore." Of course Bob, an introvert, had no way of knowing this.

"May I?" Bob asked politely, offering to fill Mary's cup with cold beer. "You most certainly may!" she replied, flashing the most beautiful smile he'd ever seen. In an instant, he fell in love. It was in that same instance that Mary decided she'd fuck him.

She stood there waiting in vain for the come-on that never came. Did he not know the sexual adventures that lay ahead for him? All he had to do was speak up. But his nerdy reticence prevented him from taking the conversation any further.

Finally, Mary shrugged her shoulders and set off in search of someone to prey upon her. She was there for the taking and Bob chided himself daily at the missed opportunity. He went so far as to practice in the mirror the conversation they would have if or when he saw her again. He played both roles, even the laughing in falsetto at the jokes he would tell. Bob was ready.

He was so ready that when he did bump into her a few weeks later, he choked. All of his training went out the window when he turned an aisle in the bookstore and stood face-to-face with the girl of his dreams. His first instinct was to run and he almost did until she smiled.

"Hey!" Mary beamed brightly at Bob. In an instant her mind scrambled to place the face. Was he the guy she fucked after the party? "You're the beer guy!" Mary laughed amused by his adorable shyness.

"That's me," the beer guy Bob chuckled, happy she hadn't asked his real name which at the moment he could not recall.

He was as nervous as a rapper in court and almost let her get away again. Almost. Bob took a deep breath and went for broke. "Can I buy you food some time? Like uh, you know, to eat," he managed to spit out.

"Sure! I'm starved. Lets go!" Mary exclaimed.

Bob forgot about his purchases and left arm-in-arm with the beauty queen and they've been together ever since.

Chapter 2

Bob and Mary doted on their new daughter like only new parents could. They bought any and everything that was even remotely baby-related. Though she was still suspect as a wife, Mary instantly turned into the perfect mother. She was attentive and traded her sporty convertible for a fully equipped mini van. Her weed and cocaine habit was replaced with gin and pills and a rather large vibrator that made up for Bob's slack.

Bob worked even harder at the firm, becoming a junior partner by Crystal's first birthday and full partner by the time she began kindergarten. His steady career advancement propelled the family in the exclusive suburb of Sugarhill, just north of Atlanta. The newly well off couple were elated when Mary became pregnant again. Both he and Mary hoped for a son, but had no complaints when Charity arrived.

"Next one will be a boy," Bob wishfully said as he held his newborn daughter.

"I'm sure it will be," Mary agreed even though she was scheduled for a tubal ligation that would ensure there would be no next one. Still extremely vain, Mary would have no more wear and tear on her still shapely frame.

They indulged young Crystal's every whim, enrolling her in soccer, ballet, gymnastics and whatever else she fancied. Some classes lasted only one session, some even less. In return, Crystal was a delightful child. Her manners were impeccable and she was obedient and appreciative. More than anything, she loved her daddy no matter what was going on. The moment dad arrived all things ceased. Bob was the center of her universe and she was his. He was delighted watching his daughter grow up.

The sun had streaked her hair to a tint money couldn't buy. It framed her beautiful face and showcased the bluest eyes most people have ever seen. Soccer, swimming, and gymnastics gave her a body to die for. She was gorgeous to say the least and she seemed to get prettier by the day. This of course disturbed her darling dad who

often saw many boys flock to his child. Even, grown men, including his co-workers, did a double take at Crystal.

Crystal's best friend Beth was equally as pretty though in a different way. Her dark hair set off her green eyes to perfection and she possessed the tall, thin frame of a runway model. The two were inseparable.

Their families became close as a result and often shared chauffer duties and hosted numerous slumber parties. The older the girls got the smaller their circle had become as the chubby, and or un-cool got weeded out from the ranks. Only their two friends, Jen and Darla survived the cut.

The topics during all of the slumber parties usually consisted of boys, music, boys, clothes, boys, sex and sex with boys. None of the girls had actually ever 'done the deed' but their sexual curiosity was certainly piqued.

"Oh my God! My breasts are so small!" Beth complained as she stood bare-chested in front of her full length mirror.

"No, they're perfect!" said Darla, slipping out of her shirt so her breasts could be inspected as well. "Mine are too big!"

"No, yours are prefect," Beth replied cupping one of Darla's heavy tits in her hand. "These are great!" After hours of giggles and dancing the girls finally settled down for the night. It was time for the main attraction. With great fan fare, Beth produced a DVD she had hidden away earlier.

"Are we ready for some good girls gone real bad?" she asked holding up the disc as if it were a sacred trophy. She put the DVD on and muted the TV so the telling moans and corny porn music couldn't be heard. The first scene consisted of a young white couple who were thoroughly inspected by the girls. The consensus was the man was a hunk.

"Oh those are so not real," Beth announced as the bleach-blond woman removed her useless bra. The large plastic breasts stood still.

The cheerful banter stopped abruptly when the well-built man stood and dropped his pants. They were in awe of the large penis dangling limply between his legs. The blonde dropped to her knees and took most of it in her mouth. She sucked, kissed and licked it until it was at full attention.

"Wow," Crystal said in amazement. It was the first time she had witnessed any sex of any kind. She was the only one. Embarrassed by the moistness in her panties, she changed her Indian style squat for a crossed leg one.

The woman lay on the sofa and spread her tan legs for the man. Crystal eagerly anticipated him fucking her but instead he attacked her with his tongue. She flailed her head to coincide with her moans as he licked her to a faked orgasm. Finally, Crystal thought as the hunk pushed himself inside of her. The girls watched as he pounded the pretty women into submission. The next scene was of a lesbian couple which both bored and fascinated all in attendance. Beth fast forwarded the action until a naked black man walked into view.

"Can that be real?!" Jen asked at the sight of the huge penis swinging back and forth.

"No way!" Beth screamed in disbelief.

"Way!" Darla replied as the two women began double teaming the dangling dick. A few minutes later the man was rock hard and as long as a forearm. He took turns damaging the internal organs of both women until he couldn't take any more.

"Ewww!" the foursome screamed as he pulled out and spewed semen on the women's faces and open mouths.

"That was so gross!" Beth spat. "And it was from a black guy!"

"Is everything ok girls?" Beth's mom asked sticking her head in the door.

Fortunately, Beth was quick with the remote and switched the channel. "Fine," they all sang together smiling brightly to prove it. She looked around skeptically, sniffing for contrabands.

"Ok then girls, lights out! We have an early start tomorrow."

"Ok!" The girls sang in unison as she backed out the room.

The girls complied and got under the covers of their make shift beds for the night.

The room was quiet except for the occasional whisper of each of them pleasing themselves. Crystal had never masturbated before but the sights of the porno were too much to bear. She had to relieve herself and did. The feeling of that first orgasm was life changing.

Chapter 3

Crystal fell in love the second she laid her eyes on Brad. He was tall, athletic, and handsome. The captain of the basketball team and quarterback had half of the female student body desiring his body.

To the dismay of his groupies, the junior had eyes for the gorgeous freshman with the blue eyes. Crystal was so excited when he asked for her number she actually forgot it. Brad had to give her his and soon after, their relationship began. It was all good until Bob found out.

"I'm not sure I like the idea of Crystal dating," Bob said pacing back and forth.

"They're kids. It's harmless," Mary said in defense. "Let the kids have some fun."

"Fun! That's exactly what I'm afraid of," he said sternly. Mary wore the pants in the family most days, but when it came to his girls, Bob didn't play. "I think I'll forbid it and tell him to stay away from her!" he concluded, nodding his head in agreement with himself.

"You do that and she'll sneak around and see the boy anyway," Mary replied thinking back to her own youth.

"I'll have a long talk with her," Bob mumbled something else unintelligible and kept pacing. The next time he passed his seated wife she rose from the bed to stop him.

"Relax dear!" She smiled as she blocked his path.

"I can't relax," he replied trying to get around her.

"Here let me help you," Mary said sinking to her knees. As soon as she got him inside her mouth he did relax. She always offered a blow job to settle a matter.

"Mmm, you think she'll be alright?" Bob moaned as Mary worked her magic.

By the time he released in his wife's mouth, he had changed his mind. "I'll go tell her it's ok, and have that chat with her," Mary said after swallowing the last of his cum.

Crystal was on the phone talking and surfing the web simultaneously when her mother knocked. "It's me dear," Mary sang sweetly before sticking her head in the door.

"Come in." Crystal smiled at her mother as she made her way into the room.

"Beth, I'll call you back later," said Crystal.

On the other line, Brad laughed. "Love you too," he said and hung up.

"How's Beth?" Mary inquired as she sat on her daughter's frilly bed.

"Great and what brings you to my humble abode?" Crystal asked sweetly, planting a kiss on her mother's check.

"I need to speak with you about the boy," Mary said plainly

"Mom, you must have forgotten. We've had that talk," Crystal laughed, "years ago!"

Mary laughed along hoping the levity would help her get her point across. "Well, we spoke about the physical act of sex, but not the emotional aspects."

"How so?" Crystal asked eagerly. Lately sex was all she could think of, but she didn't know about the emotional side.

"Boys will pressure you to go to bed with them, but you will regret it. They will tell you anything to accomplish their ends. Save yourself for marriage. Both you and your husband will appreciate it," Mary advised.

"You and dad never slept together before you guys got married?" Crystal asked incredulously.

"Absolutely not!" she replied emphatically. And she was telling the absolute truth.

Mary knew from day one Bob was a keeper and kept him. She also knew that her liberal views on sex wouldn't go over well with clean-cut Bob. Fortunately, he was will outside of the loop and never caught wind of the threesomes Mary was famous for.

Often, after Bob dropped her off from a date, she would head over to the athletes' dorm and pick a player, any player. "Your dad is the only man I've ever been with," Mary lied. She didn't regret it one bit either. It was an attempt to save her child from the degradation she suffered at the hands of so many now faceless and nameless men.

"Besides, there are plenty of ways to have fun with your boyfriend. Just use your head." Mary smiled patting her daughter's leg as she stood.

"Are you serious mom?" Crystal said elated.

"Yes dear, you're a smart girl. Use your head," Mary reiterated.

Crystal immediately called Beth when her mom left the room. "Oh my god! Oh my god!" she exclaimed excitedly. "You'll never believe this!"

"Oh my god! What?!" Beth replied just as enthused.

"My mom just gave me permission to give Brad a blow job!" she gushed.

"No way!" Beth shouted in disbelief.

"Way! She told me not to have sex but I could use my head!"

"Oh my god, Brad is so gonna love you!" said Beth. "I'm thinking about hooking up with Johnny. What do you think?" Beth was seeking Crystal's approval. Johnny was the new bad boy in school. A recent transplant to the suburbs, rumor had it he grew up in a trailer park until his stripper mom married her dentist. A star athlete himself, he and Brad quickly became friends.

Crystal screamed at the idea. "Oh my god! If you guys hook up, we can all hang out together!"

"That is so cool! Only....we don't know how to do it," Beth sighed.

"We can watch one of those movies again," Crystal said eagerly.

"Yeah and get some practice!" Beth cheered.

That weekend Crystal stayed a night at Beth's and the two spent the night watching pornos and sucking bananas. They were ready.

Chapter 4

At long last the girls would have their chance to show off their new skills. One of the cooler kids in school was throwing a party and being Brad's girlfriend got Crystal an invite. The only obstacle in her way now was her dad.

Bob and Mary were chatting in their bedroom when a hesitant Crystal rapped tentatively on the door. "Come on in sweetheart," Bob said gushing at the sight of his darling daughter. Crystal rushed over and kissed his cheek before turning to her mother.

"Mom, Christopher Johnson's party is tonight. Can I go? Please!"

"You know I don't like these parties," Bob said strongly though he had no idea what actually what went on at a teen party because he never attended one as a teen. Even in rural Ohio, teen parties were for the cool kids and Bob was never cool.

"Please dad!" Crystal rattled. "I'll be a laughing stock if I don't show up! Everyone is going. Beth's dad is letting her go."

"Bob I think we should let her go," said Mary soothingly. "She's fifteen."

"I am not sure about this Mary," Bob replied worryingly. "She's only fifteen".

"Can you excuse us a minute dear?" Mary said after turning to her daughter.

"Sure," Crystal said springing from the bed. She rushed down the hallway to get dressed for the mall. She knew her mom always got her way. She used her head.

As soon as Crystal left the room, Mary sucked her husband into submission and soon he agreed to let Crystal go to the party. Mary laughed inwardly at how easy Bob was to manipulate. Likewise, Bob chuckled to himself for faking stubbornness just to get a good blow job. Fair exchange is no robbery. Mary, Crystal and little Charity picked Beth up and headed to the huge mall of Georgia. As soon as Mary pulled the mini-van into a parking space, the girls bailed out and walked briskly towards the mall entrance. It was so not cool to be seen out in public with one's parents so they sought to put some distance between them. Mary understood perfectly and didn't complain. "Meet back here at 3pm. SHARP!" she called at their departing backs.

Once inside the mammoth mall, the girls meandered from store to store in search of the perfect outfit for their first party.

"So did you talk to Johnny?" Crystal asked as they perused the aisle of a popular clothing store.

"Oh my God, yes!" Beth gushed excitedly. "He said I'm cute, and he wants to hook up!" She was so giddy she was actually bouncing up and down

"So are you gonna do it?" Crystal wondered intently.

"Yes! And did you hear what the guys on the team are saying? They say he's got a massive cock!" Rumor had it that Johnny was extremely well endowed.

Most of the guys still considered him beneath them and insulted him behind his back. He was nicknamed T.T. for trailer trash whenever he wasn't around. Once he swung his slightly larger than average penis into the shower, he warranted the nickname "wigger" which of course meant white nigger. It was designed to be a put down, but once word spread that he had a big cock, his stock rose considerably among the female student body. And being close friends with all-star Brad gained him access to all a-list events.

"I hope Brad's cock is big," Crystal said wistfully.

"It has to be! He's so buff!" Beth exclaimed loudly. After paying for the selections with their credit cards, the girls headed over to the food court to kill time. All of the cool kids were at the mall shopping for the first big bash of the year, so it was no surprise when they ran into Brad and Johnny.

"Hey baby," Brad smiled before planting a kiss on Crystal's face.

"Hey yourself," she said dreamily from the affection.

Johnny nodded in his bad boy swagger. "Sup."

"Hey Johnny," Beth cheered stopping just short of asking him for an autograph.

"You girls ready for tonight?" Brad asked knowingly. He and Crystal had talked and he knew what was in store.

"Let's peel," Johnny said sounding bored.

"Here," Brad said extending his closed hand to Crystal. When she held out her palm, he dropped two pretty pills inside. "X," he said. "We're all takin' them. He planted another kiss on her face before departing.

"I'm not too sure about this," Crystal said wearily.

"Come on!" Beth urged. "He said 'everyone' was taking them. We have to!"

Crystal possessed her mother's good looks but inherited her father's passiveness.

"Ok," she agreed instantly.

"You girls have a good time and remember what I said. Use your head," Mary instructed as she dropped the girls off at the Johansen's house. The girls hopped out of the van.

"Thanks!" they sang out in unison.

"See?!" Crystal exclaimed.

"Oh my God! Your mom is so cool," said Beth. She was astounded at the fact that her friend got permission to suck her boyfriend's dick. How cool is that?

The Johansen's lived in a massive house in a nearby subdivision. There were cars parked up and down the street, and another lane of cars dropping off more teenagers. Mr. and Mrs. Johansen were on the front lawn greeting the kids and reassuring worried parents. As soon as they finished their welcoming duties, the couple retreated to their bedroom suite to snort cocaine, leaving the kids on their own. Beth and Crystal greeted all of their friends as they made their way inside. The party was being waged in every room of the nicely decorated home. All of the cool kids were in attendance and the girls felt privileged. They made their way into the kitchen where several kegs sat invitingly on ice. A pimpled-face boy with a metal grin handed each girl a cup of frothy beer.

"I feel funny," Crystal admitted before taking a sip from her cup.

"Me too, I'm all tingly," Beth giggled. She was giddy from the X pill they swallowed before leaving. The girls finished their beer and got a refill just as the guys pulled up. Brad had just gotten a new sports car and had made a dramatic appearance. Due to their popularity, it took them several minutes before they could make their way over to where the girls were anxiously waiting.

"Hey, Crys. Looking good," Brad said as he eyed her cute outfit. The mid-thigh

skirt was just long enough to get by her dad and still be sexy. "You too," Crystal

gushed even though he wore the same clothes he would have any other day.

"Sup," Johnny nodded at Beth sending her into a fit of giggles.

"Let's go out back," Brad suggested and turned to lead the way. He was a little buzzed and it showed in the sway of his walk. The foursome made their way outside and into the poolroom, which was as big as the double-wide trailer Johnny grew up in.

They had hoped for some privacy but found the front room occupied. A couple on the sofa was making out so furiously they didn't even acknowledge the intrusion. They tried the first room but that was taken by another couple having sex. Brad closed the door after watching a few strokes and tried the next door.

"In here," he ordered finally finding an empty room. They settled on the bed and Johnny produced

a joint. The girls watched as he lit it and took a deep drag. He passed it to Brad who did the same. Brad grabbed Crystal's face and cupped his mouth over hers. She inhaled slowly as he exhaled the marijuana smoke into her mouth.

Meanwhile, Beth readily smoked the joint when Johnny passed it to her. Brad and Crystal never broke their lip lock and began making out. She felt her panties soak as Brad groped her all over. Crystal peeked over to see what Beth and Johnny were doing on the other side of the bed. She watched them make out as Brad clumsily sucked on her breast, seeing first hand that the rumors about Johnny were true as he removed a long hard penis from his jeans. Beth did not hesitate in the least and headed south. She took him in her mouth and worked his cock just like the girl on the DVD. When Brad stood up in front of Crystal she knew it was her turn. She was about to use her head. Afraid to look, she closed her eyes and opened her mouth. Brad rubbed the head of his dick on her wet lips before easing himself inside of her mouth. Slowly he slid in, moaning as he filled her mouth. Crystal told herself to relax. She didn't want to gag once he was all the way inside. She opened her eyes suddenly when she felt his pubic hairs tickling her nose. He was finally in but was only halfway down her tongue. Brad had a baby dick. Crystal pulled back to look at it and wanted to cry. It was three, maybe four inches long and as wide as two fingers. Brad pushed himself back inside and humped her face.

Since his dick was too small to apply any of the techniques she learned from the porn star, she just remained still. It didn't take long before his knees buckled and his tiny penis pulsated as he came in Crystal's mouth. Disgusted, she pulled away and watched as a dribble of semen ran out of his dick. Brad grunted as he slumped onto the bed, within seconds, he was asleep. Crystal looked over at her friend who was having the time of her life. She envied Beth, as she sucked and stroked Johnny's long dick. Suddenly, she gagged and pulled away as he erupted in her mouth. Johnny locked eyes with Crystal as he stroked himself, sending semen into the air. They both knew that she would soon be on the receiving end of his cock. The three of them smoked another joint and shared a beer as Brad snored. Crystal could only shake her head at her sleeping boyfriend. She fought the urge to cry.

"Here girls, this is for tomorrow," Johnny said handing both of the more x-pills.

"What's tomorrow?" Crystal asked eagerly as she accepted the pill.

"He invited us to the lake!" Beth chimed in enthusiastically.

"My mom's husband has a boat," Johnny added as Beth's cell phone began to chime.

"It's my dad," Beth said before taking the call. "We'll be right out." Crystal could only sigh again as she looked at a comatose-like Brad while Beth and Johnny made out once more.

"See you tomorrow," Johnny told Crystal intently as they left the room.

"Looking forward to it," she smiled shooting a glance down to his crotch. The seeds had been sown.

Chapter 5

As soon as Crystal took Beth's call the morning after the party, she regretted it. Her bestie launched into hysterics about the night that she'd rather not recall.

"Oh my god! Oh my god! Was that cool or what!" Beth screamed, and then continued until she ran out of breath.

"Well, at least you had a good time," Crystal said regrettably. She sighed. "That makes one of us."

"Tell me you didn't chicken out," Beth said seriously.

"No, I did it but..."

"But what?! What? Tell me you went through with it!" Beth demanded.

"I did it... but... Brad has a tiny cock!" Crystal blurted out. "It's miniature!"

"No way!" Beth shouted. She could not fathom that the starting quarterback, star of the track and field team, all star 1st baseman did not have a big penis.

"Why?" Crystal whined wishing it wasn't true. "It was almost gross."

"You know maybe it was because he drank so much!" Beth offered. "Johnny told me they had quite a few drinks before they came to the party. He probably couldn't get it all the way up!"

"You think?" Crystal asked with newfound hope. "Yeah, that's probably it huh?"

"Totally! I mean Brad is too buff not to have a big one. We still on for the lake today?"

"For sure! Just have to get permission first," said Crystal. "Hopefully."

"The lake! With a boy?" Bob demanded when his daughter came to him seeking his permission. The truth was he was fine with it. He had recently met Brad and was thoroughly impressed with him even going

16

so far as calling him a fine young man. He figured he would protest a little bit and maybe get some head out the deal.

"Baby, excuse your father and I so we can discuss this," Mary said taking the bait.

She sucked an approval out of her husband before going to check on the girls. Beth was over and they were trying on bathing suits. They giggled at the frumpy suits they wore for their parents' benefit, while the skimpy bikinis were hidden in a bag.

"Hey girls," Mary sang and peeped in. "Your dad said it was fine. Have a good time."

"Thanks Mom and don't worry. I'll just use my head," Crystal assured her confused mother.

"Well... ok dear have fun," Mary said backing out of the door just as Brad sounded his horn from the driveway.

Brad was all teeth when Crystal slid in behind him. He didn't remember the blowjob, but Johnny assured him he got one. "Hey babe," he said leaning in for a kiss."

"Hey yourself," a beaming Crystal said after getting her tongue back.

"Hey Brad. Where's Johnny?" Beth asked thirstily from the back seat.

Brad laughed at the panic in Beth's voice. "He's at the lake already. Chill out!" he joked. He turned to Crystal. "Sorry about last night. I drank one too many."

Beth tapped Crystal's shoulder to indicate she was right all along. "Well you better make it up to me today!" Crystal demanded. She intended to hold him to his promise to eat her out.

Johnny was working on top of his stepdad's house boat that was docked at Lake Lanier. Both girls admired his tan muscular chest as they approached.

"Welcome aboard," he greeted cheerfully, "You guys ready to have some fun?"

"Definitely!" they yelled out together as only close friends could.

And what fun the two couples had! After dropping the anchor in the middle of the lake, Brad and Johnny raced jet skies with the girls as passengers on back. Then, they frolicked in the murky water until they were all exhausted. The foursome was worn out by the time they finally made it back to the boat, but Johnny had an answer for that as well. After passing a cold beer to each of his guests, Johnny dumped a pile of white powder on the table.

"That's what I'm talking about!" Brad exclaimed as his buddy made thin snortable lines on the table.

"What is that?" Beth asked eagerly but while she was eager, Crystal was frightened. Something about the glistening white powder unnerved her.

"It's one hundred percent pure, Columbian fresh scale cocaine," Johnny replied grossly overestimating both its purity and origin.

It was fifty percent at best and straight out the Peruvian jungle, only to be stepped on ten percent each time it changed hands. Johnny leaned forward and inhaled a line in each nostril which seemed to propel him backwards into the sofa. "Fuck!" he exclaimed, wincing from either pain of pleasure.

Either way Crystal decided she wanted no parts of it. She frowned as Brad greedily inhaled two lines before popping yet another bottle of beer open. To her surprise Beth dove in and snorted half a line up each nostril.

"Don't fuckin chicken out!" Johnny urged. Snort the rest of that shit!"

"It burns!" Beth giggled rubbing her nostrils. She snorted the rest anyway. What happened next really amazed Crystal. It was as if she watched herself lean forward and snort the remaining lines.

Johnny refilled the glass table several more times as they partied while Brad continued to drink nonstop. He had switched from beer to whiskey and the effects were showing. He was pissy drunk by the time

Johnny escorted Beth to one of the bedrooms. Crystal had to practically drag her drunken boyfriend to the other. The second they stepped into the room, Brad fell onto the bed and began to snore at once. Crystal wanted to cry but instead went to retrieve another beer. Why not get drunk too, she mused. From the main room, she could hear Beth moans emanating from her and Johnny's bedroom. Curiosity got the best of her and she inched towards the cracked door to sneak a peak. Johnny had both of Beth's legs high in the air and was vigorously eating her out. She was moaning and flailing her head until she announced that she was "cumming." The orgasm shook her friend so hard, Crystal swore the boat moved. Her bikini bottoms were soaked from the display. "My turn," Johnny proclaimed. He lay on his back with his dick standing at full attention. Beth wasted no time in getting him inside her mouth.

Crystal was envious watching Beth suck Johnny off. It looked so fun she was tempted to barge in and help. She stood there and imagined it was her slurping loudly on the long penis. Johnny grunted signaling that he had reached his peak but Beth didn't budge. She took it all like a veteran cock sucker, something she was in fact on her way to becoming. Frustrated by the display on so many levels, Crystal grabbed a half joint from the table and retreated to the top deck. She did cry this time until the soothing effects of the weed engulfed her. That was her first realization that drugs not only made you feel good, but they could make you feel better too.

Johnny, unable to wake Brad, ended up driving the girls' home. When he pulled into Crystal's driveway, she bolted from the car and ran inside without saying goodbye. Later, Crystal ignored Beth's first ten calls before she finally answered the phone. Once again, she immediately regretted it as Beth exploded into her ear.

"Oh! My! God!" Beth yelled. "I have never come so hard in my life! She went on for several more minutes, detailing each aspect of her sexual romp. "Ok, ok. So tell me. How was Brad?" Beth asked eagerly. "Details!"

"His tongue is magic!" Crystal lied. She was preparing to ad lib the great oral episode when Beth dropped a bomb on her.

"Johnny said he's ready to go all the way with me. He said he loves me!" Beth said giddy from the 'L' word.

"So are you?" Crystal asked sharing her friend's enthusiasm.

"Am I! I am so ready!" she said.

"Me too. I'd do it with Brad," Crystal said wishfully. She would too if he would just stay sober enough to fuck her.

"Ok. Ok. So we're all going back to the lake next weekend and it's on!" Beth said excitedly. "It's going down next weekend." However, when the next weekend arrived, the only sex Crystal came close to were the sounds of Beth and Johnny in the next room. Brad had puked his guts up before curling up around the toilet and going to sleep.

This time Crystal found solace in a whole joint from Brad's pocket. Armed with it, and a fresh beer, she went up top to relieve herself. She was halfway through both when a shirtless Johnny appeared in all of his tanned splendor.

"Hey you," he said plopping down into a lounge chair.

"Hey ya self. Where's Beth?" Crystal inquired as she passed the joint.

"Sleep." He chuckled triumphantly, knowing he put her to sleep. "Here, try this," he said handing a small pill to Crystal. She took it without question and popped it in her mouth. She washed it down with a swig of beer.

"X?" she inquired, lucky it wasn't cyanide because it was already dissolving in her stomach.

"Nah, it's a Xany," he answered. "It'll take you there and it goes good with weed or coke," he explained like some professional drug abuser. Crystal was already feeling the effects of the weed and beer and let her eyes run lustfully over Johnny's body.

Johnny saw the look in her eyes. "You like?" he asked seductively.

"Here you are!" Beth said joining them on the deck. She straddled Johnny. She looked around for a second. "Where's Brad?" she asked.

"Sleep," Crystal replied dryly.

Beth laughed wickedly. "You dirty dog!" Johnny whispered something in her ear that made her laugh even more wickedly.

"I'll ask her," she giggled looking into Crystal's blue eyes, almost lustfully.

"Ask me what?" Crystal asked. She was hoping, nearly praying, Beth was going to ask her to join them for a threesome. It would be just like the porno DVD, but with Johnny as the star. But before they could ask, Brad stumbled deck side and ended the fantasy. He was staggering from all the intoxicants already in his system, but he still popped open another beer.

Crystal was so livid once she got home, she withdrew from the world. No phone, no text, no chat, no social networking. Instead, she focused her attention on her younger sister who was delighted to be recognized. Charity had been unintentionally neglected once puberty hit.

On Monday morning, Crystal entered school to a throng of long faces. Some people were crying. "What's wrong? Who died?" Crystal half joked. She was a teenage girl too so she knew they could get emotional over next to nothing. Jen pulled her back and looked deeply into her friend's face.

"You haven't heard? You don't know!" she asked astounded.

"Heard what? What are you talking about?" Crystal was becoming worried.

"Brad. He wrecked his car Saturday. He's dead," Jen said. "Brad's dead!"

The next thing Crystal knew she was surrounded by people standing over her.

"Give her air," one called out. Followed by "Someone get the nurse." As the details came out, Crystal learned that that Brad was three times

over the legal limit when he slammed his car into a tree at a high rate
of speed. Both he and his new vehicle were folded almost completely in
half. Brad, the love of her life, was instantly killed and dead at
sixteen.

That is until Black stood up and a massive lump ran down his leg. "Come on shawty," he said leading her into his plush bedroom. Crystal was appalled at the thought of blowing the huge black man but sobriety was far more distasteful or so she thought.

"Take yo shorts off," he demanded as he dropped his own.

"I thought you just wanted some head," Crystal winced.

"Nah, I'm tryna fuck too," he said whipping out a huge penis.

Crystal complied and disrobed. She sat naked at the end of the bed. When Black stepped forward, she closed her eyes and opened her mouth as wide as she could but it wasn't wide enough. Black couldn't fit any more than the head of his massive member inside of her mouth. Crystal grabbed it with both hands and desperately stroked it. She was trying her best to get him off before he tried to put it inside of her. To her horror, the more she stroked, the longer and thicker the gigantic dick grew. Black pushed her on her back and clumsily fondled her vagina with his fingers.

Black marveled at her young tight body. She was a far cry from the rundown white girl one stumbles upon in the hood. By the time you usually get a white girl, she has been run through the wringer. He ran his large pointer finger in and out of her before getting ready to enter her. Again, he was only able to get the large head of his penis inside of her. Still he humped as Crystal screamed. It felt like he was pushing her insides each time he made a short thrust. Luckily for Crystal, the sight sounds and smell of the pretty white girl was too much for him to bear. Black stood up over her stroking himself and began spurting thick globs of hot semen all over Crystal. Her chest, neck, face and hair were drenched. After regaining his composure, they dressed and went back into the front room. Black grabbed his bag of dope and fisted some out. "Here," he offered handing her a small rock.

"Huh?" Crystal curiously asked the paltry offering.

"That's the going rate for pussy 'round here' he exclaimed. The look on her face spoke volumes and sent him back into the bag.

Chapter 6

Crystal was a wreck. She secluded herself in her room and her parents became concerned.

"May I come in?" Mary asked after softly knocking. When she didn't get a reply she ventured slowly inside. "How are you feeling dear?" Mary neared for a reply but Crystal pulled the comforter over her head and turned away.

"Dear, the funeral is today. Aren't you going?" she asked taking a seat on

Crystal's bed. The word funeral slammed the reality of Brad's death home once again. Crystal moaned loudly and began to sob.

"Oh my poor baby," Mary cooed and scooped her daughter into her arms. She joined her in her grief and cried along with her. "I know baby, I know. Let it all out."

Mary held her child tightly. She was so relieved that Brad only killed himself, and had not taken anyone else along with him, especially Crystal.

"Here, take this," Mary instructed, pressing an oxycontin pill to Crystal's lips. "This will help ease the pain. Now get a bath and get ready. It's important that you be there."

Crystal showered slowly in the scalding hot water. She hoped the sting of the scorching water would replace the ache in her heart. It didn't. It wasn't until she began to towel off that the effect of the pill was felt. It felt like she had smoked some weed followed by a line of coke. Mary was right, it did ease the pain.

Brad was a popular star athlete which meant a huge turnout for his funeral. Crystal sat with the family, locked arm-in-arm with Brad's mom. They accepted sincere condolences from herds of people who came by offer them. The minister preached a sermon laced with the warnings of indulging in life temptations and about the tragedy of a life cut short and salvation. After the sermon, they all filed out of the church and made the slow procession to the gravesite. Crystal was overcome with at the sight of Brad's casket being lowered into the ground. Her knees buckled and if not for Brad's dad, she may have collapsed. They all watched solemnly as hundreds of mourners filed past the grave, dropping a single rose onto the casket. Once the last flower was dropped, Crystal turned away. She would not watch dirt being tossed on her beloved.

Crystal found Beth and Johnny waiting by his truck. Beth took off, slammed into her and squeezed. The two girls sobbed as they rocked back and forth. They could have stood there like that forever had Johnny not intervened.

"Come on. Let's get out of here," he suggested, guiding the girls to his truck.

Once they were all seated in the cab, Johnny handed them both a pill and a beer from a cooler behind the bench. Neither girl asked what they were taking and instead swallowed the pill with beer and awaited the effects. "Let's go party," added Johnny as he started his truck.

"For Brad." They rode in a sad silence until he pulled in front of a large, well-appointed house.

"My mom and her husband are in Florida. We got the whole place to ourselves," said Johnny as he led them inside. They settled onto the huge leather sectional in the dark yet beautiful den. Ever the host, Johnny handed the girls fresh beers and lit a joint. He turned on the massive TV and an almost life-sized couple appeared. The woman was in her thirties and had a pair of fake boobs that were near perfect. The pudgy older man was moaning loudly as she blew him. The display bordered on the line between interesting and gross. The woman turned around and the out of shape fifty-something year old man took a few strokes into before collapsing on top of her.

"That's my mom and stepdad," Johnny giggled pushing the display firmly into the gross category. He replaced the DVD with an updated porn featuring a well-endowed white guy having his way with two busty black girls. "I have something that will make you guys feel better." he said.

Crystal hoped he meant his dick, but when he went into the adjacent room to retrieve it, she knew it had to be something else. He returned a minute later and sat a well-used glass pipe on the table. Johnny began chopping small pieces off a small rock. He put one of the chips on the pipe and handed it to Beth. She looked frightened but when Johnny put the flame of the lighter to the tip, she inhaled slowly. Beth eyes grew large as she inhaled the sizzling smoke. He repeated the process with Crystal and she too inhaled yet another drug into her system.

The girls took turns smoking the tiny chips until they were gone. Neither girl asked what they were smoking nor did they wonder why Johnny didn't smoke any himself, but they were instantly high. He knew that crack would have prevented him from the erection that was growing in his pants. Besides, he had plenty left. Johnny and Beth began kissing passionately as Crystal watched on. "Come on," Johnny invited hoarsely. Crystal looked to Beth who nodded approvingly. She and Johnny began to kiss as Beth pulled his erect dick from his pants and into her mouth. When Crystal saw it, she pushed her friend out of the way and swallowed half of his cock.

Beth was almost jealous at how much of Johnny her friend had in her mouth.

Johnny pushed her head down as he hit the small red record button on the remote that lay in his hand. The girls licked and sucked Johnny until he pulled away causing the best friends to kiss each other. He stripped them both as they kissed and then laid Crystal down.

"Go ahead," he ordered and Beth buried her face in Crystal's crotch. Crystal came within seconds of Beth's tongue touching her. Johnny rushed inside of her and stroked her virginity from present tense to past. The threesome had threesomes for the rest of the night, only breaking occasionally to get high.

Bob and Mary decided not to question their daughter when she returned the next morning. They were content that she made it home safe and sound. Crystal walked past her parents and straight upstairs to her room. Remembering how good the pill her mom gave her made her feel, she snuck into her medicine cabinet in search of them. Mary had a ton of pills and it took a minute to find what she was looking for. She dumped half the contents into her hand and put the bottle back in its place.

Crystal popped one in her mouth and washed it down with water. Once she settled into her bed, the warm feeling of the narcotic engulfed her and she drifted off to sleep where she dreamt about sex and drugs, the new staples in her life.

Chapter 7

After the night of the funeral, Crystal began sleeping with Beth and Johnny on a regular basis. He always insisted Beth go down on her friend and he always taped it. His house had become the hang out spot so he had compiled several hours of sexual trysts.

The other constant thing was the drugs. Crystal would snort, smoke or pop whatever he had to offer. It wasn't too long before Johnny had the girls chip in on the dope.

Most days two hundred dollars, sometimes more, went towards Johnny's drug of choice. Crack Cocaine. Soon, all three were hooked on the powerful drug. Some days smoking took the place of sex mainly because Johnny couldn't get an erection once he started using.

He got his dope from a dealer in the ghetto of North Atlanta. Black, as he was called, stood six feet two inches tall and weighed a prison-toned two-fifty. He wore his nappy hair in sloppy dread locks and had a mouth full of shiny gold teeth. Black obviously got his name from his complexion because he was the darkest human being Crystal had ever seen. He lived in a run down apartment complex that surprisingly had several nice cars parked in the beat up parking lot. The girls hated going inside with the black man who openly gawked at them, but sitting in the truck in that area was asking for trouble.

"Sup," Black drawled as he let them in his apartment. The outside was shit but the inside was decked out in a ghetto fabulous décor. He had every electronic device and gadget in the small room, and a state of the art flat panel TV dominated most of one wall.

"Sup Black," Johnny said slapping the man's large out-stretched palm.

"Chillin' shawty. Anytime you and your lil' friends feel like partying y'all holla at me, ya hear?" Black said looking at Crystal's creamy legs. "We're cool." He stood back and examined the girls' money. After completing the purchase, the threesome retreated back to Johnny's house and smoked the night away.

Mary's pill supply took up the slack between Crystal's get high sessions. After depleting the OxyContin, she tried the Xanax and then experimented with others in search of a buzz.

"Have you been using my pills?" Mary demanded barging into Crystal's room.

Crystal was far too high from whatever blue pill she had just taken to argue so she just denied knowing what her mom was talking about. "And how dare you come in without knocking!" said Crystal. "Dad!"

"Something is very wrong. You're not yourself," Mary said sincerely. She was concerned about the subtle changes she noticed. It had been months since Crystal went shopping yet she still demanded money, more now than ever.

"Nothing is wrong with me! Now please leave!" she shouted. The yelling alerted Bob and he came to investigate.

"What's going on ladies?" he asked from the doorway.

"She's accusing me of stealing her pills, that's what's going on!" Crystal yelled at her bewildered father.

"All of my meds have disappeared," Mary complained.

Bob looked at his daughter and refused to believe she could be using. He didn't like the fact that Mary kept so many different pills in the first place. "Come on. Let's get to the bottom of this," said Bob, guiding his wife out of the room. "I'll be back to speak with you young lady!"

Mary had used enough drugs in her life to know something wasn't right. Crystal's focus had changed. Something was different. "We have to keep a closer eye on her, she is getting older. More Temptations," Mary advised. Bob agreed but then turned right around and bought Crystal a new car for her birthday. With her own set of wheels, she was free to come and go as she pleased.

Her cravings for sex and drugs convinced her to start seeing Johnny without Beth. Beth stumbled across a raunchy sex video featuring just the two of them and got revenge. Using Johnny's own computer while he slept, she uploaded the video to all the social sites and then advertised it, far and wide. It went viral and by Monday it was the only topic of conversation in the hallway.

Crystal confronted Johnny in the cafeteria and tore into him. "How dare you put out a fake video of me?!" she screamed.

"Fake? Nothing fake about my cock in your mouth," Johnny shot out to the amusement of on-lookers. "Besides I'm not the one who posted it. Why would I?"

"Because you're a piece of shit trailer trash bastard is why!" she shot back.

"This coming from the village whore! Get the fuck away from me slut!" Johnny said sending more chuckles around his table. He was suddenly very popular now and was holding court with the cool kids. Crystal was very popular as well. A video confirming that she sucks dick shot her stock through the roof. Had it been an I.P.O, she would have been rich.

Crystal survived on whatever pills she could score but she still spent a lot of time sober. She needed the rush of the hard drugs she had gotten used to. It was that "need" that navigated her car to North Atlanta. She was terrified to get out of the car when she reached Black's apartment complex. However, the yearning agreed to escort her up the steps. The door opened shortly after her tentative knocks and there stood

Black, in all his ghetto glory. He was shirtless, and the heavy gold chain stood out brilliantly against his black skin.

"Sup shawty." He frowned as he looked past her. "Where's John boy?"

"Um, I needed to get something. If it's ok," she stammered still standing in the doorway.

"I don't sell shit unless you call first!" Black boomed

"I'm...I'm sorry," Crystal stuttered fearfully, fearful that she wouldn't be able to cop.

"Imma let it slide, this time!" he said stepping slightly aside so she could enter. He kept enough of his massive body in the doorway so she would have to squeeze against him to get through.

Once inside, she handed him two hundred dollars sending him into the next room. He returned a few seconds later with a quarter ounce of ATL's finest crack. Crystal's eyes widened at the large amount of dope in the baggie

"Your boy Johnny been shortin' you, huh?" Black laughed flashing his gold teeth.

Crystal didn't respond, but the dealer was right. Johnny had been producing half that amount for their money. Black gave her his number and told her to call first next time, nor she wouldn't get served even though he would never turn away her money, or any money, for that matter.

Crystal got home to a small commotion in the house. It seemed Mary had somehow misplaced two hundred dollars. "It has it to be in my purse," she insisted.

"I'm sure of it." She checked under the sofa cushions.

"You'll find it. Be patient," Bob advised joining in on the search. But unless they planned to drive over to Bolton Road and dig into Black's pocket, that money was gone.

Crystal pretended to help for a few minutes until the drugs in her purse insisted on being smoked. She was headed upstairs when Bob called the search off.

"Just take my ATM card. The code is Crystal's birth date," he said handing the plastic over to his wife.

It took a few days for Crystal to smoke all of the drugs, but as soon as she exhaled the last of it she went in search for more.

After entering her birth date, Crystal withdrew two hundred dollars from her father's account. She called Black and went to cop. This went on for weeks until the card came up missing. Bob absolutely refused to believe Crystal had taken his card, or the fifteen hundred dollars missing from the account. He suspected Mary had an uncontrolled shopping spree before his daughter. It wasn't until the bank's surveillance camera showed a clear picture of Crystal that he finally had to accept it.

When mother and father confronted their child she denied it and a huge fight ensued. Mary and Crystal yelled back and forth as Bob tried to referee and participate. Finally, Crystal got up and stormed out.

"Let her cool off!" Bob said exhausted from the battle. "We'll talk to her when she gets back in."

Crystal was in no mood for her parents' crap. It had been several days since she was able to use anything and it was killing her. She noticed she was speeding out of anger and eased her foot off the gas pedal. Black's number was on her speed dial now and it only took a press of a button to get him on the line. She advised she was on the way to cop and he agreed. What she neglected to tell him was that she was penniless.

"The usual?" Black asked pulling out a large bag of crack cocaine.

"Yes please. But I won't be able to pay you today. I'll need some credit," she said very reasonably. But Black wasn't reasonable and he did not do credit and he told her so. "Shit shawty we don't do no credit 'round here!" he exclaimed, putting the bag of drugs back down.

The look of desperation on her face spoke for itself and Black could hear it in her voice. Besides being fluent in Ebonics, he also spoke desperation, quite well in fact. "I can let you work it off," he offered feeling a stir in his loins. He would pay top dollar for a romp with the pretty little blonde-haired, blue-eyed snow bunny.

"Work? Ok," Crystal agreed eagerly though she had never did any work ever in her life. For some reason, washing dishes and other odd jobs ran through her mind.

"Here you go, lil' mama," he said giving her the full amount she usually purchased. "You know I'ma wanna hit that again!" Crystal snatched the dope and pulled her pipe out of her small purse. She was prepared to take a hit on the spot until Black stopped her.

"Whoa! You can't hit that shit here!" he demanded. "Take that shit home wit cha!"

Crystal limped to her car, sore from the sexual beating she just took and sat gingerly inside. Black watched proudly knowing he caused that limp.

A police officer who was parked in the lot also watched her leave Black's house. He decided to give the young girl a pass even though he knew she had drugs and knew where she bought them. Both Black and the cop decided to approach the car when they saw Crystal's lighter flicker as she took a hit. Black backed off once he saw the cop

and returned back into his lair.

Crystal was arrested and charged with possession of drugs. She was taken to the precinct where she was fingerprinted, stripped, searched, and photographed. Her photo would be unrecognizable to anyone who knew her. She looked like a stranger with her blood-shot eyes and semen-matted hair. To make matters worse, the cop startled her when he knocked on the car window causing her to cough up the hit before completely inhaling and feeling its full effects. She never got a chance to enjoy the drugs purchased with her body and dignity. As if all of that wasn't bad enough, Bob and Mary had just arrived.

Chapter 8

Bob and Mary paid the five-thousand dollar bond and claimed their battered child. The forty five-minute drive from the ghetto to the suburbs was made in complete silence. Both parents stole an occasional glance at their wayward daughter in the mirror. Mary wondered where they went wrong. Where they failed. They arrived at the house and filed solemnly inside. "Get some rest dear. Busy day tomorrow." Mary said wearily, looking at her daughter for the first time.

Crystal nodded and limped up the steps. She took a long shower attempting to wash away the shame and degradation. The same emotions all addicts go through when sober, until the monkey kicks in that is. The semen washed easily away, but her vagina was too sore to be touched. As distasteful as it was, she had to leave it for another time. After the shower, Crystal vainly searched her room for something, anything to take the edge off. After finding nothing, she finally just cried herself to sleep. The sleep was not a restful one, and Crystal tossed and turned until dawn crept into her window. Mary wasn't far behind it.

"Get dressed. We leave in twenty minutes," Mary said sternly from the doorway. "You'll need a few changes of clothes so pack a bag." Mary's tone left no room for haggling so Crystal quickly complied. Still far too sore to put on jeans, she found a pair of sweat pants and topped it off with a t-shirt. She packed an overnight bag with clothing and toiletries.

"Are you hungry? We can stop and grab something," Bob offered as Crystal descended the stairs. He was still unable to look at his daughter but his tone was compassionate. Stop on the way to where, Crystal wondered but didn't ask. Instead, she shook her head no despite actually being quite hungry.

The family minus Charity, who spent the night at a friend's, rode in silence. The only voice heard was that of the navigation system giving turn by turn directions to the still unknown destination. Bob turned onto a shaded tree-lined driveway and stopped at a guard's shack. The sign above the gate read "Shady Oaks" a name Crystal was vaguely familiar with.

"What is this place!" Crystal demanded after her father's muted conversation with the guard gained them access.

"This is where you can get some help dear," Mary replied pleadingly.

"Help for what! I don't need any help!" Crystal spat out as her agitation grew.

"You have a drug problem and need rehab," Mary shot back

"Rehab? You're fucking crazy! I'm not going!" Crystal shouted.

Bob slammed on the brakes. The sudden stop sent the women forward, testing the restraints of the seat belts. He turned around and pointed a trembling finger at his daughter as he spoke. "You listen here young lady. You have been using drugs and God only knows what else. You have lied to us, stolen from us and you will complete this program," he yelled.

Crystal bowed her head submissively and cried silently. Meanwhile, Mary was quite impressed by the show of machoism. She planned on fucking him the second they got in.

Bob parked and led the procession to the facility's intake area. "Standard procedure," he explained when Crystal hesitated. She stood over the guard as he fumbled through her bag. He looked to be in his early twenties and under other circumstances she would have thought he was cute. He smiled up at her holding a pair of her panties and inhaled deeply as if savoring the aroma. "Having fun?" she spat.

Mary turned to look back but the guard dropped the panties and she missed the exchange.

"First door on the left," the intake receptionist said pointing down the hall. Bob led the way and tapped on the open door.

"Come in," a forty-something black woman smiled. Mrs. Hall was pleasant and pretty with a touch of gray in her thin well kept locks that were pulled into a tasteful bun. "Have a seat," she said. She pointed to the chair facing her desk.

"Thank you," Bob and Mary replied. They took their seats with Crystal between them. "Why are we here?" Mrs. Hall asked looking at Crystal.

"Because my parents made me," Crystal hotly shot out.

"And why would your parents force you to come to a drug and alcohol treatment center?" she asked evenly. "Do you use drugs and alcohol?"

"I got arrested with some crack," Crystal said avoiding the real question.

"And do you use crack cocaine?" Mrs. Hall asked tilting her head slightly.

"I got it from that nigger and..."

"CRYSTAL!" Mary yelled embarrassed for the black woman. "Apologize to Mrs. Hall this instant!" "That's not necessary," said Mrs. Hall, raising her hand to halt the apology. "I hate niggers too! Most black people do. There is a difference." Still, Crystal bowed her head and offered an apology. She was ashamed by her outburst and said so.

"That's fine," Mrs. Hall smiled, "We'll have plenty of time to talk later." I'll be your counselor so we'll get to know each other quite well. Go get settled in and get some rest."

"How long do I have to stay here?" Crystal pleaded to her father.

"Until you're better," he answered, looking towards the floor. He knew if he looked at his daughter he would lose his resolve and take her home.

"It's a sixty day intensive course. The results are up to you. Some people come many times before they get in right," Mrs. Hall advised. She pressed a button on her phone that summoned a "yes" from the receptionist over the speaker.

"Have Carl come escort our new guest to her room please," Mrs. Hall ordered.

The pantry sniffer appeared at the door seconds later to escort Crystal away. As they walked towards the residential wing, Carl checked out the new guest and was quite pleased. "What are you looking at?" Crystal said when she caught him giving her a 'once over'.

"A very pretty young lady," Carl replied with a smile.

"Do you sniff everyone's underwear?" Crystal asked.

"Only the cute ones." He laughed.

"Creep!" she frowned.

"Hey, be nice. I'm a good friend to have in here. Two months is a long time. You may need me."

They reached the room before Crystal got a chance to formulate her next quip. Carl knocked on the door and waited for a reply.

"Come in," a small voice called from inside. Carl turned the knob. "Hey bay..." the pretty red-headed girl began but she cut off the affectionate greeting upon seeing Crystal.

"Kathy, this is your new roommate Crystal. Crystal, Kathy," Carl said making the introduction. "I'll leave you girls."

"Great," Crystal said sarcastically as she entered the room. "Hey Kathy."

"Call me Kat and welcome to Shady Oaks," she said with a pretty smile.

"Thank you," Crystal said dryly tossing her bag onto the empty bed. "So what brings you here?" Kat asked.

"My parents," Crystal said.

"No!" Kat giggled. "I mean, what drug?!"

'I got caught with some crack and got arrested," Crystal replied.

"Crack? Really?" Kat frowned, shrugged and continued. "I'm here for Meth this time."

"This time? How many times have you been here?" Crystal exclaimed.

"This is number three!" said Kat without the slightest trace of shame. "Two months, and out! Nothing to it, plus it helps me through."

"I'll bet," Crystal said under her breath. "How old are you?"

"I'll be sixteen in two months," Kat answered. "You?"

"I'll be sixteen too," Crystal replied lying on the unmade bed. The next thing she knew Kat was waking her for lunch. "Hey, sleepy head! Time for lunch!" Kat sang as Crystal blinked her into focus.

"Huh?" she said putting her surroundings back in order. "Yes I'm starved." "Well let's go," Kat cheered. After washing her face and freshening up, Crystal followed Kat to the dining hall. She was impressed with how luxurious the place was. It reminded her of her wealthy grandparents' country club. Shady Oaks however cost far more than any country club. Bob's insurance company was paying two hundred dollars a day for the stay.

Crystal delighted in the huge salad bar, making a master plate of fresh fixings. She ordered a tuna melt while Kat opted for a cheeseburger and fries. They both filled their glasses with diet cola from the fountain and found a seat.

The other patients were old or young but all white and wealthy. Kat was bouncing in her chair and talking a mile a minute between bites of the burger. Crystal recognized her behavior was from either a xany or oxy and she wanted one. Her parents brought her here for a help and a Xanex would definitely help.

After the meal, Crystal borrowed one of Kats swimsuits and followed her to the pool. Not surprisingly, Carl was poolside taking in the sights. "Hey girls." Carl smiled as they entered the indoor pool area. Crystal pretended not to hear him and slipped into the warm water.

"Hey Carl," Kat yelled out flirtingly and then joined her friend in the pool.

"What's his deal?" Crystal frowned watching the guard stare at them. "What is he? Some kind of pervert?"

"Who? Carl!" Kat asked stunned, "No he's cool. He's a good friend to have in here."

"What exactly does that mean?" Crystal asked. Kat shot a conspiratorial glance around the pool before answering. "I'll tell you when we get back to our room," she whispered.

Crystal held her to her word and asked the question again as soon as they got back into their room. "He can bring us, stuff," Kat said producing a couple of xanys.

Crystal plucked one from her palm and gulped it down.

"Can he bring me some crack!" she asked eagerly.

"Crack! No. Stinks to bad. Plus that stuff is for niggers and trailer trash." Kat said popping her own pill.

"Is not!" Crystal said defensively, still very faithful to her drug of choice.

"Sure it is," Kat shot back. "You just got caught with crack and they dropped the charges. If you were a nigger, you would be in prison. NOT Rehab!"

"Dad said they will drop all charges once I complete this program." Crystal added.

"See! We're rich white girls! We get probation or rehab. Only niggers go to jail and only niggers smoke crack!" Kat re-iterated. It was the most Crystal had heard the N-word used in her life. Kat was obviously a racist, but kids in her own neighborhood were far more tolerant. Her friend Darla was dating the black point guard at their school and no one salted an eye.

"Besides, meth is so much better!" Kat proclaimed. "Better? Than crack?"

"Way better! It lasts longer and you don't have to go into the ghetto and risk getting shot in your head by some deranged nigger! Or raped. Those niggers love white girls you know!" Crystal felt a stab of pain at the remark thinking about Black and that lead pipe he called a dick.

"Plus you can snort it, smoke it, lace it or even shoot it," Kat went on, singing the praises of methamphetamines until Crystal was convinced.

"So can you have Carl bring us some?" She asked excitedly at the prospect of this wonderful drug. "He won't bring that in. His ass is scared! He'll only do pills," Kat sighed.

"Oxy?" Crystal beamed knowing that would take the edge off for sure. "How much will he charge?"

"Ten for a blow job or twenty for some pussy," Kat replied matter-of-factly. "But don't worry. He cums super quick."

The course began Monday morning just after breakfast. All clients were given a drug test that most failed due to the large amount of drugs that got them there in the first place. They took physicals administered by the medical staff, followed by evaluations by the psychiatric staff. Blood work and I.Q. test were done until lunch. After lunch, the group watched graphic movies about the effects of drugs on the mind and body. Then they all went their separate ways until later in the evening when they meet up for group therapy.

Crystal and Kat sat in the back and cracked jokes as patient after patient got up and spilled their guts. They paid close attention when a pretty girl close to their own age stood to talk.

"Hey ya'll. I'm Mandy," she said in a deep southern drawl that tick-led Kat immensely.

"Hey Mandy," the group called back.

"I'm here because I'm an addict. I was using Crystal Meth everyday and it destroyed me. I ended up selling everything I could to get my hands on it, whether it was mine or not." she said without pause. "When that failed I even sold my body."

Crystal was so tuned in she almost missed Kat slip out the back. Curious as to what she was up to Crystal followed her out. She saw her duck into an office marked security.

Crystal quietly cracked the door open and saw Kat giving Carl a rather professional looking blowjob. She figured either Carl didn't have much dick or Kat was a sword swallower because she had her face flush against his crotch. She returned to the meeting just as Mandy finished her speech. Kat was close behind her and reclaimed her seat. The girls joined the applause along with the rest of the teary-eyed group. Had Crystal stayed, she too would have cried and her story could have ended right here. Back at the room, Kat crushed a few of the pills and snorted them with her friend. It wasn't meth but it would do. High as a kite, the girls giggled until dawn.

"It's gonna be a long day!" Kat griped as the sun popped over the horizon.

It was a long sixty days but they made it through. Crystal looked great and felt better. She may not have beaten her drug addiction but thanks to Kat and other veteran addicts, at least she learned how to better conceal it. Now it was time to see what all that meth talk was about.

Chapter 9

Crystal's stint in rehab ended two weeks before school was set to begin. It was her junior year and she intended to regain her prestige. Mary understood her daughter had a point to prove and said nothing about the revealing clothes she chose to buy as they shopped. It was nothing too outrageous. Just enough to let her peers know that she was a force to be reckoned with. Johnny's sex tapes got him in a bunch of trouble since most of the girls were sixteen and seventeen. That, in the state of Georgia, constituted child pornography. His step daddy, a dentist bought him probation and sent him to live with a man, who was widely believed to be his biological father.

Neither Beth nor Crystal would swallow their pride and the two remained estranged. It didn't matter because she still had Kat, and Kat had pills. Crystal did learn how to get through an entire day sober if she had to. That was something that she was unable to do before rehab. Now she would fix herself a stiff drink and take a hot bath. Occasionally, she would masturbate if she were feeling particularly antsy. She got a job at the mall over her dad's objections. He wanted her to take an internship at his firm, but Mary thought she needed to be around kids her own age. It cost her a blowjob for her to get her way and Crystal got the job. The small kiosk she worked for was owned by a handsome Kurdish man named Kamal. It sold handcrafted jewelry made by relatives in his native Iraq. It only paid ten bucks an hour but Crystal wasn't there for the pay.

The mall was like a physical Facebook. You had mall friends and 'liked' everything they said. It was the place to see and be seen. An added incentive was that Crystal's new bestie Kat also worked in the small space and with her steady supply of mood altering pills, the jewelry kiosk was the happening booth in the bustling mall. Crystal had fully filled out and was stunning. Not a day went by that droves of men didn't vie for her attention.

Likewise, Kat, although smaller turned out good as well. She was very pretty and her bright red hair was a sexy contrast to her green eyes. She only popped pills these days. Kat bedded a new guy almost weekly, but Crystal was still reserved. She hadn't had sex since the incident with Black and his flagpole. The attention began to get to her and she knew it was time to get laid. She viewed every boy who approached as a potential lover. However, her next lover would not be a boy at all. Kamal was a grown man. Both Kat and Crystal adored and flirted with the handsome olive skin-toned man. He only came through once or twice a week and his wife who made no secret of her distrust and disgust of the two young girls.

As fate would have it, Kat called in sick on the same Saturday afternoon that Kamal visited his business alone. Crystal found every reason to squeeze past him in the small space. She made sure to slowly grind her ass against his crotch when she did. By the third time he was rock hard and Crystal pressed her ass into it. "Mmmm. I'm sorry," she said seductively. She eyed his stiff crotch. "Did I do that?"

"Be careful little girl," Kamal warned seriously. "Do not bite off more than you can chew!"

"I don't bite. I swallow," Crystal said causing her boss to close shop for the day. The next thing she knew she was in the passenger seat of Kamal's Mercedes speeding towards a nearby motel. He pulled a vile of coke out and snorted a hit up each nostril. Crystal took the vile when it was passed and quickly snorted it before common sense had the opportunity to speak up.

"Remove your clothing," Kamal demanded once the door closed behind them.

He quickly stripped and shoved his erection in her face. Crystal gave him the blowjob his wife would never do. Arab women were no match orally to Americans. Kamal only lasted a few minutes inside of her mouth. Luckily for Crystal, he quickly regrouped and fucked her to several orgasms of her own. The two lovers got together as often as his multiple businesses would allow. At least once a week for the next couple of months, they got high then got low. Crystal wasn't the least bit surprised when her period didn't come. Kamal was livid when he found out and blamed her. He gave her a thousand dollars and fired her at once.

"You should tell his wife!" Kat fumed. "He's a grown man. That is so not cool!"

"I'm responsible too," Crystal said solemnly. Getting pregnant was bad enough but her coke connection was also out the window. "Well, that's me," Crystal sighed after her name was called. She took a deep breath, went into the sterile room, and had an abortion.

Chapter 10

Senior year arrived and Crystal found herself to be focused and sober. As impossible as it would seem to her admirers, she got even prettier. She fielded prom offers from the first day of school. Crystal looked oddly at her phone when Beth's number appeared on the screen.

"I miss you so much," Beth blurted. "I can't believe I let a boy come between us!"

"Me too! I'm so sorry," Crystal admitted as the tears began to flow. The old friends spent most of the evening on the phone catching up. By the time they got together the next day, it was as if it had only been a few days that they were estranged.

It was just like old times. And those old times consisted of coke and threesomes. This time the lucky guy was the super cool Christopher Johnson. The place where the girls shared their first sexual experience years back with Brad and Johnny became the stage for drug-fueled orgies.

The cocaine stirred something in Crystal that she fought desperately to control. She even found herself driving towards Atlanta to Black's apartment a few times but fortunately she always managed to abort the mission before getting there. It was also fortunate that Mary was liberal with her valiums. Mary never used crack herself but could vividly recall yearning for the powered cocaine for years. She's would even yearn for it now if she let it.

One Saturday afternoon, Crystal was desperately and at her wits end. Beth was on an out-of-town shopping trip and she had no one to hang out with. On a whim she hit up Christopher in hopes of any relief of some sort. "Hey Crystal. Christopher is out of town," Mr. Johnson said cheerfully over the phone. He had met her several times at his house over the past few months. Once, he even walked in on the kids snorting cocaine and to Crystal's surprise, he bent over and inhaled a line of his own.

"Oh. Well, ok," Crystal sighed heavily, trying to figure what she should do next.

"My wife is also gone. If you would like you may come over," he offered in that sexy Eastern European accent of his.

Crystal wasn't sure why she agreed but she did. She took a refreshing shower and dressed in a sexy under clothes. When she pulled up to the spacious house she paused and reflected. There was no doubt in her mind that she was about to go fuck the father of the boy she had been fucking. Mr. Johnson appeared at the door with a smile that erased her second thoughts and invited her in.

"Hello, young lady," he greeted punctuating it with a kiss on her cheek. The kiss reverberated throughout her

entire body causing her lonely vagina to quiver.

There was no doubt about it now. Mr. Johnson was about to get some pussy!

"Hello, Mr. Johnson," Crystal said shyly.

"Ian please," he corrected as he led her into the den. "So, I will fix you a drink, no?"

"Fix me a drink, yes," she giggled.

Ian returned with a bottle of wine and a joint of the strongest weed Crystal had smelled or smoked in her life. "I have some free base, would you like?" he offered causing a reaction in Crystal's body.

Every cell in her body remembered the rush and feeling of grandeur caused by cocaine. The demons she had been dodging surrounded her and demanded she say yes. And she did.

"Sure," Crystal said barely above a whisper yet loud enough to set her host in motion. He must have ran because seconds later he returned with a silver tray containing crack and all the fixings. A crack kit if you will, complete with a pipe and

butane torch. "There is not much so you may indulge," he offered as he prepared a

nice sturdy hit. He handed her the loader pipe and lit the torch.

Crystal closed her eyes and inhaled the hot steam of smoke. He fixed a few more hits until the small amount was exhausted.

"We make love now, no?" Ian asked eagerly.

"We make love now yes!" Crystal cheered. The couple stripped in no time and maneuvered themselves into a sixty-nine position. Since they started together it was only fair they finish together both cuming in each other's mouth.

Ian next introduced her to anal sex and literally fucked the daylights out of her. She felt so good she didn't realize how much trouble she was in. Crystal fought and lost the battle with Ian and crack for the rest of the school year. They met up once or twice a month at a distant hotel and did the deed. He always brought crack that he wouldn't smoke and always fucked her in the ass, always.

Luckily for Crystal, the entire Johnson clan went to Austria for the summer. That meant Bob finally got a chance for his darling daughter to intern at his firm. She was so busy learning the exciting world of law there was little time for anything else.

Crystal made up her mind that summer that she intended to follow in her dear dad's footsteps. She was going to study law.

Chapter 11

"And that's where your father and I met," Mary said as she pointed to a building Bob had never been to. The proud parents were giving their freshman daughter a brief tour as they took her to her dorm.

"That's the quad. Some of the best parties were held there," said Bob, pointing to the building he and his wife had actually met at.

"There, dad!" Crystal exclaimed upon seeing the sign of Jennings Hall. It had been built after Bob and Mary's tenure so they were unfamiliar with it.

The females rushed inside empty-handed leaving Bob to tote her belongings. Luckily for him, her car loaded with clothes was still at home. They found the room and were taken aback at the couple already there helping their child. It was well known that Crystal was going to have a roommate, they just didn't know she would be black.

"Oh!" Bob exclaimed as he re-checked the number on the door. "This is room 112?"

"Here we go!" The pretty girl's pretty mom said sharply.

"He meant nothing we..." Mary began in defense of her husband.

"Hi, I'm Keisha," the co-ed interrupted sweetly reaching for Crystal's hand.

"Crystal," She shook Keisha's hand, ending the awkward moment created by the adults. Keisha was very pretty and very light, only a few shades lighter than Crystal. She had curly hair that was the same golden hue and hung over of her eyes.

Seeing the girls hit it off so easily caused the apprehension to dissipate instantly. After unloading the first load of freshman needs, both parents bid their children farewell and retreated back to the suburbs.

"You know my parents aren't racist. They're just..."

"It's cool. My parents are," Keisha laughed. "Not in a hate whitey type of way but just sensitive, almost paranoid
about it."

"Well, I'm sure we'll get along just fine," Crystal said with a smile as she unpacked.

"Hey if you need the room for your boyfriend or anything just let me know," Keisha reassured. "No worries there. No men for me."

"Oh!" Keisha perked up even more. But you're so pretty."

"Thanks but I've sworn off men, for a while anyway."

"Same here," Keisha said. She began to change. Crystal was awed by her flawless yellow skin. She had a stunning figure, featuring full breasts and a round ass that protruded from her skimpy panties. Keisha caught her staring and laughed knowingly. "Yeah we'll get along just fine."

Crystal dove head first into her courses and was at the top of her class. Her desire to succeed curbed her desire for drugs. She just kept herself too busy to entertain anything else. Not to mention Keisha often expressed disdain for drugs and drug users. That killed the occasional thought of asking if she knew where to score some drugs.

She did well but it couldn't last. It didn't. Crystal talked herself into going to one of the campus parties. Hearing so much about the quad, even from her mom, she decided to check it out. One beer led to another and soon Crystal had a decent buzz. The ok looking guy she was dancing with leaned in and made her an offer she couldn't refuse.

"I got a little coke," he said and off they went. When he said he had a little coke he was not exaggerating. She inhaled the lot of it in two lines. "Hey! You didn't save me any!" her host griped.

"That's all!" Crystal exclaimed in disbelief. It was barely enough to wet her whistle. The door was opened and she wanted to know where she could get more.

"Yeah, we snorted most of it earlier," he explained. "That's it. It's over."

"Thanks," Crystal said sarcastically and stood to leave.

"Hey! Don't go! I was hoping we could...you know," he said patting his bed.

"I got my period," Crystal lied and hit the door.

"That's ok. I'll take some head!" he called after her just as the door closed. The paltry amount of coke had Crystal's demons stirring again. She needed some relief of any sort and she needed it quickly. As she walked briskly across the campus to her dorm, her mind raced from face to face.

She was still undecided when she reached her room, until she walked in that is.

There was Keisha fresh from the shower in all of her light brown glory. "Hey Crys!" she beamed as her buddy entered the room. She went back to applying a wonderful smelling lotion to her blemish-free skin. When she saw the lustful gaze that Crystal locked on her legs, she dropped the towel that was covering her luscious body. "A little help?" She asked extending the frilly bottle of ointment to Crystal.

It took a second for Crystal's mind to process the statement because she was stuck on her roommate's body. The perky brown nipples that topped her prefect C cup breasts down to the tuft of curly brown pubic hair amazed her.

"Hmm? Oh. Yeah ok," Crystal agreed and began massaging the lotion into her firm legs.

"Mmmm, that feels good" Keisha purred softly.

"It does." Crystal agreed working her way up her thighs. Keisha lay on her back, closed her eyes and partially spread her legs. It was a posture of submission telling Crystal she could do what ever she wanted to her.

The first thing she wanted to do was touch the fat brown pussy. When she did, it got instantly wet all over her fingers. That, of course, was an invitation to slide a finger inside of it.

"Mmm," Keisha moaned and contracted her tight muscles on Crystal's finger, holding it inside of her. Crystal was first surprised when her own face lowered towards the swelling vagina. She was twice surprised that her tongue was on a woman's vagina. And then again at how sweet it tasted. Keisha moaned and reacted to every flick and lick from Crystal's tongue. It only took a couple of minutes before she came loudly. Crystal came just as loud once they changed places and Keisha returned the favor.

As they lay in the post orgasm glow, she craved for more. The door was opened and she wanted to get high. Keisha noticed a slight change in her roommate's demeanor and assumed it was guilt. She had been a lesbian long enough to know some chicks felt funny after eating pussy for the first time.

"Hey it's no big deal, you know. You got curious and we had a good time. Don't sweat it," she comforted.

"Huh? No, it's not that," Crystal replied distracted. "I just need to earn some extra money."

Bob and Mary tightly controlled the purse strings. They knew full well that spare cash meant spare temptation. Their daughter had already dodged a huge bullet and they had to be cautious.

"Well my brother manages a strip club. I don't know how you feel about stripping, but with your body you would make a killing!" Keisha advised.

After a week of fighting temptation, Crystal finally relented. "Call your brother."

Chapter 12

It took a few agonizing days for Keisha's brother to call back but when he did, he told them he was en route to take Crystal to an audition. Keisha did her best to show her some of the latest dance moves but she fumbled through. "Don't worry you'll be fine," she said finally giving up. Dance moves or not Crystal was a knock out.

The black patrons who frequented Damian's club would love her. Crystal answered a knock on the door and pulled it open. There before her stood one of the must handsome men she had ever seen. Not handsome for a black, but handsome period. Damian was tall and obviously muscular under his expensive clothes. He had a head full of curly light brown hair and golden eyes embedded deeply in his yellow face. "Um hellooo!" he chuckled, breaking the spell his good looks cast upon her. He was equally taken with her.

"Oh, I'm sorry! You must be Damian," Crystal said. She smiled brightly and let him in.

"And you must be Crystal," he said licking his chops.

"And...she is a special friend of 'mine'!" Keisha warned. It was their code for him not to fuck her.

"I got you, I got you," he chuckled as he led Crystal away to her audition.

Crystal was impressed when he led her to a new BMW and opened the door for her. Instead of taking her to the club he pulled into underground parking of a high-rise mid-town building.

"What's here?" she asked curiously as he pulled into his reserved spot.

"This is where I live," he answered. "I figured you might wanna hang out," He held the door open to let her out.

"What about my audition? The job?" Crystal asked. "Oh you go the job already," he said eagerly and led her to the elevator. Crystal nodded approvingly at the swank apartment and took a seat on the plush suede sofa. "Can I get you anything? Beer, wine, weed, coke?"

"Coke!" she blurted out before the question could dissipate from the air.

"Soft or hard?" he asked raising an eyebrow. He was praying hard. That would make his job so much easier.

"Well, I've never tired it hard," Crystal lied answering the twisted prayer.

Damian fought the urge to pump his fist and yell "yesss!" Instead, he calmly went to his stash and got his supplies. He had to stifle a laugh as Miss Never Tried Hard expertly broke off a piece and loaded the pipe. She flicked the lighter and inhaled more problems into her short troubled life.

"You won't tell Keisha about this, will you?" she asked urgently after finally exhaling the noxious smoke.

"As long as you don't tell her I fucked your brains out."

Deal!" she laughed sitting the pipe and lighter down.

Damian led her to into his equally decked out bedroom and immediately began to disrobe. Crystal didn't budge as the painful memory of Black and his monster cock flashed in her mind. To her delight, he revealed a light brown, pretty penis. It was big in its semi-erect state but not abnormal. She rushed out of her clothes to get as naked as he was.

When Damian lay on his back in the center of the bed, Crystal knew exactly what he wanted. There was no reason to haggle and she put him in her mouth. When he grew stiff inside of her mouth she pulled it out to marvel at it. Damian knew she had to be clean if his sister was fucking her so he pulled her around for a sixty-nine. Damian found the rumor of white girls giving the best head to be completely true. She made him explode in her mouth sooner than he thought possible. He was so turned on by the pretty white girl he stayed hard and entered he doggy style. In his line of work, he got a lot of pussy but rarely was it as tight as Crystal's. Before he could stop himself he came again inside of her. He mused to himself that he hoped Keisha didn't plan on eating her pussy tonight because it was full of his cum.

Damian fucked her a few more times in between letting her hit the pipe. When he was thoroughly spent, he took her into his shower to wash away the evidence. He gave her just enough crack to ensure a call the next day. And call she did, everyday. He sexed her crazy for weeks until it was time to put her to work. Crystal was hooked on the dope and he knew he owned her.

"Look, I am having second thoughts about putting you in the club," he said, beginning a calculated sales pitch. She pulled his dick out of her mouth and asked why.

"I think you would do better as an escort. The pay is better and I'll be able to spend more time with you," he said affectionately.

"Ok," she replied and went back to work at her blow job. The next night she sucked a strange man's dick for money. Crystal was now officially a call girl.

Chapter 13

Crystal began servicing several clients every night. Although Damian was charging a thousand dollars or better for a romp with the pretty white girl he only gave her a few hundred a night and a nightly supply of crack. Just enough for the night, just enough to ensure a call first thing the next morning. Her busy night life clashed drastically with school so she stopped going to class all together. Another down side was she and Keisha fell out completely. The relationship had deteriorated to the point where they didn't even speak and Crystal didn't even care.

One night Keisha brought home a pretty white girl and sexed her right in front of her. It turned Crystal on so much she masturbated along with them. It was no surprise when Crystal was summoned to the Dean's office. They informed her that since she had been dropped from all her classes, she had to vacate the dorm.

No worries because that's exactly what Damien had hoped for. He put her up in a nice condo not too far from his own. He went over there everyday to get his dick sucked and make sure she ate and maintained her weight. With her increasing drug habit, he had to keep an eye on her. As much as his clients loved her he would force feed her if he had to, intravenously if necessary.

In return for food, lodging and dope, Crystal would fuck and suck the daylights out of whoever came to the apartment. If you were there it was because Damien sent you, after you paid him you could do virtually anything you want, once inside. A couple times a week, Damien sent a voluptuous black girl over to help with the threesomes. Crystal could not believe her good fortune. Sex, drugs, money. What more could she ask for? She was loving life.

She got a good scare one day when she opened her door and saw Mr. Klein standing there. He was a co-worker of her father's at the firm. Mr. Klein lusted secretly the whole summer that she interned. A cou-

ple of times the sexy little outfits she wore forced him to lock his office
door and masturbate. "You?" he asked incredulously.

"Damian sent you?" she asked worried about her parents for the
first time.

"Um, yes. He told me he had a new girl! Never in my wildest
dreams would I have dreamt it was you. And I've dreamt of... Well this
is a pleasant surprise."

"It's a surprise alright," she sighed stepping aside so he could enter.
Thirty minutes later he emerged happier than he'd ever been in his
life. He became a regular at least once a week. Not only was he paying
Damian a thousand dollars but he always left a hundred or two on the
coffee table on his way out. Crystal's neighbor, an elderly lady, watched
men come and go for months. She noted that the men were old, young,
black, white and one Asian fellow. She timed their visits and recorded
a license plate or two when she could.

To make matters worse, Damian cursed the neighbor out once or
twice for asking too many questions. Mrs. Pounds made it a point to
record his license plate number too. The nosey neighbor had logged
thousands of hours watching cop shows and knew something was
amiss. She called the local precinct to report the nefarious comings and
goings. She was no stranger to the police and was not taken very serious.

After all this was the same lady who reported seeing President Oba-
ma breaking into cars a few weeks back.

The officers still played the 911 tape to amuse themselves on slow
days. "I knew we couldn't trust him!" she said triumphantly as she reported the leader of the free world was stealing car stereos. Eventually,
one of her calls did catch the attention of the newly promoted Sergeant
Harper who insisted that someone check out her claims.

Out of spite, he sent the thorn in his ass that was Detective First
Class Milner. Milner sat with the extremely talkative old lady one day
and did see some unusual traffic. Not the quick cop and go traffic that

signaled drugs were being sold but the steady flow of various types of men. It was enough to spark the veteran cop's interest. He came a couple of days in a row and saw it wasn't a fluke. Something was being trafficked out of unit 52. When he spotted well-known drug dealer and pimp Damian

Wells, he nodded with satisfaction. He was almost giddy at being able to nail the elusive bad guy on something. The elation was short-lived when he watched the prettiest girl he had seen since his own daughter was alive. The streets had claimed her a few years back, choked to death by the man she was dating.

Milner seethed as he watched the couple enter this luxury vehicle and speed off. He made a vow then and there that Damian was going down. By any means necessary. Unable to secure a warrant, the detective decided to move on his own. Dressed in a cheap suit and doused in cheap cologne, he knocked on the door. Most of the men, who came and went, literally were either young 'rapper' types or serious-looking business men, and the cop didn't resemble either. He actually gasped when Crystal opened the door. She was pretty from the distance he had first observed her, but up close she was stunning.

"Yes, can I help you?" she smiled brilliantly flashing her electric blue eyes.

Milner forgot what he was supposed to say once he got caught in those azure pools.

"Damian sent you?" she asked sounding slightly puzzled.

"Um... yeah um, Damian," he stammered as he entered the nice pad. "So how does this work?"

"You paid the man, so I'm yours. Any way you like. Well almost," she giggled.

She wore a half-open oriental style robe that showed half her breast and was short enough to show half of her round ass. Detective Milner considered quitting his job at that moment. He was torn between doing his job and wanting to touch this beautiful creature.

His dick was so hard it hurt. It strained against the cheap fabric of his slacks dying to be set free. Desperately needing contact with the woman, being married for twenty-five years without once being unfaithful was quite an accomplishment. However, when the robe came open the streak had come to an end. It was with a heavy heart that the middle-aged man fucked the young woman. He didn't last long and minutes after entering her, he slumped over still inside of her.

"Um...excuse me?" Crystal finally said after enduring his weight for several minutes.

"Oh I'm sorry," Milner said rolling off of the small girl with a grunt.

Crystal slid from under him and into her tiny robe. The way she rushed urgently into the next room alerted the detective's senses. Do your job, the cop admonished himself as he reached for his discarded underwear. He decided not to wash the combined fluids off, saving it as a reminder.

After quickly dressing he went to break the bad news to Crystal. He entered the room with his badge held high, to find her sucking feverously on the pipe. "Excuse me," Detective Milner announced. "You are under arrest. Put the pipe down and get dressed."

Crystal coughed up the hit she just took and choked severely. "Really! Are you serious right now! You fuck me and now you wanna lock me up!" she spat furiously.

"I'm doing my job," he offered apologetically.

"Your job?" Crystal fumed. "Is it your job to fuck me?" She berated the stubborn cop to no avail. When that didn't

work, she tried another tactic. "Please don't do this to me," she pleaded. "My parents would die. Please. I'll suck your cock!" The offer of head gave the detective pause.

How long had it been since Mildred blew him. "Look, it's Damian I want. You help me get him and you'll

go free," he offered.

Crystal wasn't smart enough to be afraid of Damian and quickly agreed.

Technically, she was still under arrest even though she rode cuff less in the front seat of Milner's vehicle.

"You told her what?" Sgt. Harper boomed when the detective filled him in on the deal. He was well aware of his subordinate's desire to cut white girls loose while showing no mercy to blacks.

Harper hated the pimps and pushers as much as anyone but felt they were parties to the crime as well. They were the ones who fucked and sucked for money. Just because they were dumb enough to give all their proceeds to a funny dressing negro didn't make them any less culpable. "So what about the four grams of rock cocaine?" Harper asked.

"The pimp is the supplier. We can make a buy of a couple of ounces and nail his black ass on a trafficking charge!" Milner said enthusiastically.

Harper decided to let the "black" remark go agreeing that Damian was indeed a bigger fish. Still, he wanted to make the detective beg. He knew the man loathed answering to a young black man, boss or no boss.

"Besides Sarge, she's a good kid. Her parents will freak if they find out she was whoring for some black pimp," the detective said sympathetically.

"Black pimp as to opposed what a white one?" Harper spat. In truth, he was just as racist as his counterpart.

"That's not what I meant!" Milner began in a futile attempt to clean it up.

"Well that's what you said. Go make the deal. Get out of my office!" As soon as Milner left the office to make the call to set Damian up, Sarge made a call of his own.

Crystal urged Damian to rush over with two ounces of crack for some girlfriends from school. It was an unusual request, but Damian, like a lot of dealers, went with greed over common sense. Common sense dictated that Crystal wouldn't just suddenly have someone from school who urgently needed two whole ounces. Greed told him to get the quick two grams. When the drug dealing pimp pulled up, he was stalked by at least ten police officers. The one posing as a gardener discreetly keyed his walkie-talkie, alerting the team to his presence.

"Where your friend?" Damian asked finding Crystal alone in the living room.

"They are coming back. They left the money though. Did you bring the stuff?" she asked nervously. Again, her demeanor gave him pause but again money was more important.

"Right here," he said tossing the bag of dope on the coffee table in front of him. "Shit you may as well hook a brother up." Damian went for his zipper.

"Just a sec, let me grab the money," said Crystal rushing to the rear. The swarm of police, led by Detective Milner, almost knocked her over as they rushed out of the bedroom to make the arrest. Damian was leant back, stroking his dick in preparation for the blowjob he just ordered.

"What the fu..." was all he got out before he was tackled and hand cuffed.

"You're under arrested you low life, pimping bastard." Milner said once he safely secured the cuffs.

"Arrested? For what? Where's Crystal?" he demanded. "Bitch you gone get yours!"

"Add terroristic threats to the trafficking, and pandering charges," the detective said triumphantly. Crystal wept silently as she rode back with the elated cop. It was bad, but it was about to get worse. Back at the precinct she gave a full, graphic account of her drug use and prostitution.

Bob and Mary wept on the other side of the two-way mirror as their daughter laid out all the sordid details. It became too much for Bob and he opted to go wait outside.

As soon as Crystal finished the sordid statement, she was free to go.

Chapter 14

On the way home, Bob gave in to his daughter's demands to stop at her condo. He wished he could burn down the building that accommodated her prostitution. He needed something or someone to blame. The police let him look upon Damian handcuffed to a desk in an interview room. That provided no relief. He had expected some flamboyant black man with a lawyer suit and matching high-heeled boots and perhaps a lavender hat with a feather extending out of it.

But no, Damian was a regular looking guy. He looked like one of the blacks in the sub-division or at the office. Even though she knew she left Damian in police custody, she still rushed about the unit as if he may pop in at any second. She had amassed quite a bit of clothing and accessories. The closets and drawers were stuffed. Knowing she had only one trip, she chose the cream of her clothing crop and stuffed them into bags.

She rummaged through her nightstand, moving aside lubricant and other sexually related items. At the bottom of the kinky accessories she found a small piece of crack.

Crystal's mouth began to water as she picked the poison up. She could hear it sizzle, flirting to be smoked as she walked. She walked triumphantly to the toilet and flushed the piece away.

When they arrived at the house, Bob sent the women inside and had himself a good cry in the garage. Once he got that out of his system, he hauled the bags inside.

"Where is she?" he asked when he found Mary sitting alone in the den.

"I sent her up to her room to rest. Busy day tomorrow," she replied, before sipping her wine. The next day was a busy one indeed, yet a familiar one. The same stoic guard checked his list against a driver license before lifting the gate to Shady Oaks. Again Crystal had to speak with Mrs. Hall as part of the intake process. Only this time she was contrite and non-combative. Mrs. Hall was sweet, compassionate and understanding as she consoled her.

"Nothing at all to be embarrassed about," she began. "Feel blessed you made it back at all. Two of our former patients died from drug overdoses. You're a survivor," she cheered.

Crystal was relieved to see that her roommate was a middle-aged woman from the suburbs. Claire had been forced into the program for her penchant for painkillers.

"My husband sent me for help," she quipped sarcastically

"Well, that was nice of him," Crystal offered.

"Meanwhile, he's helping himself to our Spanish maid!" Claire said ruefully. "It's ok cuz I've helped myself to our gardener Juan. Not a word of English but he can eat a taco like nobody's business!"

This time there would be no pills to take the edge off. No short cuts. No bull shit. Crystal was determined to reclaim her life and stay clean. The meetings she once scorned she now embraced and participated in whole-heartedly. Once she built up the nerve, she stood up and shared some of her own painful experiences with the group.

"Hey, my name is Crystal" she began then paused to grace the audience with her bright smile. "And I'm a drug addict."

"Hey Crystal," the room greeted as one and cheered her on. "My drug choice is...well...excuse me was crack cocaine," she said proudly placing her addiction in the past tense. The group cheered again. Crystal left out the sordid and embarrassing details as she spoke, recounting just how far down the drugs had taken her. The entire room was in tears by the end of her speech.

Bob and Mary visited their daughter faithfully, staying the entire allotted time. Young Charity wasn't allowed to visit, nor did she know there was a problem. Crystal apologized profusely and begged for their forgiveness, which of course they gave. Her parents assured her it was not her own fault. They placed the blame on Damian, the drugs, and even themselves. The first stint in rehab had been dreadfully slow. This time the sixty days elapsed so quickly, it both amazed and frightened her. Claire saw her hesitation and understood the problem. She knew it well since this was her forth ride.

"Buck up young lady!" Claire demanded. "You're gonna be just fine."

"You think?" Crystal asked eagerly. She was feeling needy and wanted to be reassured.

"Sure! If I had your attitude, I would have never come back," Claire said matter of- factly. "Now let's get out of here. I can't keep Juan wait-ing."

Bob and Mary were parked out front and smiled broadly as their daughter emerged from the building. The reunion was cheerful although all parties were concerned. All three of them prayed this rehab would stick.

Chapter 15

At the exact moment Crystal was waving her goodbyes to the staff and acquaintances at Shady Oaks, Damian was standing in front of a superior court judge. He just pled guilty to one count of possession with intent to distribute. Milner and his comrades were furious that the D.A. reduced the trafficking charge and dropped the pandering charge all together.

The Assistant District Attorney claimed he couldn't put Crystal on the witness stand because she was drug addict and prostitute. Damian's name was not on the lease and the drugs were found on the table not on him. He agreed to plead guilty for a split sentence of five years with only one to serve, with good behavior. Damian would be pimping again in six months.

It cost him twenty grand for his lawyer as well as offering Jasmine's services for free to the eager D.A. Even with the sweet deal, Damian was seething and vowed revenge. The fact that one of his girls had crossed him ate at him. It had to be addressed and dealt with severely enough to prevent it from happening again. He may not have owned a lavender suit but Damian was a true pimp and intended to check his hoe.

Damian sat in the county jail for a few months waiting to be shipped to the overcrowded Georgia prison system. Since the state prisons were packed to the gills, they had to release some people just to let others in, and Georgia did not like releasing people. Every night he would pull out picture of a smiling Crystal and plot. He eagerly looked forward to the day when he could plunk those electric blue eyes out of her pretty face. Finally, his name was called to be transferred to prison.

After a month of diagnostic testing, he was assigned to a cell where he would serve out his time. His release date was now only four months away. He entered the cell and nodded a 'What's up' to his new cellmate. The huge black man with gold teeth and a shiny bald head nodded back from the top bunk. As Damian unpacked his belongings the man checked him out contemplating on whether he was going to rape him or not. Once he got settled in, he got on his bunk and retrieved Crystal picture.

"See where I'm at?" he asked Crystals smiling face. "See what you did to me?"

"Say what, shawty?" the big dude asked leaning down.

"Nothing, talking to this picture," Damian replied. "Lil' bitch set my ass up and got me knocked off."

"Shit, me too shawty. A bitch got me in here too," he said with a golden grimace.

"White girl I had working for me put the police on me. Got me knocked off with a couple ounces," Damian said.

"Me too!" the bald man said animated. "Damn white girl told on me and got me a trafficking charge."

"Here she go," said Damian handing the picture up to his new friend.

"Get the fuck outta here! This the same bitch!" he said practically yelling.

"You know Crystal?" Damian asked incredulously.

"Yeah I know her trifling ass." He growled. "By the way, my name is Black".

That night after he had sex with Crystal, Black watched her limp to her car. She wasn't the first to leave crippled by his monster cock. He saw Crystal about to smoke and was about to chase her off but the cop got to her first. She wasn't the first customer to be thirsty enough to sneak a blast in the parking lot before heading home. He would always run them off knowing it drew heat to him.

When Black got arrested the next day, he just knew it was Crystal who put the police on him. He was wrong of course but had no way to know otherwise. "Been down three years and six months!" Black told Crystal's picture. At the moment, he changed his mind about raping

Damian. "Say shawty? Do me a favor, wait on me before you get her, please!" he pleaded.

"That's what's up," Damian agreed and an unholy alliance was formed.

Chapter 16

Rehab had ended as summer began which gave Crystal a chance to spend some time with her little sister. Charity was thirteen and filling out by the second. Bob and Mary were delighted to have Crystal there to issue stern warning about drugs and boys.

Charity adored her older sister and listened to her admonishments. With no option in the matter, Crystal went back to work at her father's firm. She protested adamantly but was unable to provide a valid reason.

Of course saying "Dad I tricked with freaky ole Mr. Klein once a week oh and likes to lick butts" wasn't the best idea. Crystal decided she would just ignore the man. Sure he had his way with her when she worked as a prostitute but now she was an intern. Mr. Klein would not be ignored. He did everything short of hiring a circus to get her attention. Whenever he walked into a room she walked out. It worked for a while until Klein couldn't take it any more.

One day he caught her in the copy room and eased up behind her. He looked around to ensure no one was looking and grabbed a handful of her ass.

"Are you crazy!" Crystal hotly inquired as she knocked the man's hand away.

"Yes! About you!" Klein chuckled easing forward.

"Is there a problem here?" a deep voice demanded from the doorway. It was Dave, one of the law students who clerked over the summer.

Dave was tall, handsome, and obviously protective. He and Crystal had shared a few flirtatious glances but never spoke. "There is no problem. Go back to sorting mail or whatever it is you do!" Mr. Klein said dismissively.

"I was talking to the young lady," Dave replied not moving an inch.

"This creep is harassing me," Crystal complained sliding behind Dave.

"Just a little misunderstanding," Klein chuckled. "Everything is fine, just fine."

"Good. Let's see to it that this doesn't happen again. I'm sure Crystal's dad wouldn't appreciate further misunderstandings!" Dave commanded.

Klein tucked his tail as he slinked away leaving the couple to an awkward silence except for the sparks

flying between them.

"That guy is such a loser!" Crystal fumed.

"I see," Dave agreed, shaking his head. "By the way, I'm Dave."

"Crystal" came the reply accompanied by a batting of the eyes. "But I guess you know that."

"Yeah I do actually work with your dad. Great guy!"

"Oh you don't have to say that for me to go out with you," Crystal said pressing the issue. The shyness returned and Dave lowered his head. Crystal wondered why all the good ones were shy but obnoxious losers were always in your face.

"I'm sorry. I didn't mean to offend you," said Crystal apologetically.

"No! Um... I ... well, you think...can we go out. To eat?" Dave stumbled on the way to the first date.

"Sure!' Crystal exclaimed. "As a matter of fact, I'm hungry now."

Dave and Crystal went on what was the first of many lunch dates. The reticent Dave managed to open up and steal Crystal's heart. She found his shy demeanor refreshing and endearing. Dave had drive, goals and plans. After a few dates, Crystal decided she wanted to be included in on those plans. It was she who suggested they go on a real date. She decided to seal the deal with some ass.

When Dave came to the Atkins residence to collect Crystal for their first date, Bob was delighted. He shook the young man's hand so heartedly it unnerved him. Bob chatted him up until Mary broke in so the couple could leave. Bob hated to see them go and half-entertained asking if he and Mary could double.

"You guys have fun," Mary urged as they headed for the door. Bob came over and put his arm around his wife to watch their departure.

"Fine young man," Bob announced proudly as he thought of his work ethic.

"Fine indeed," Mary agreed looking at his ass.

Dave took Crystal to a trendy Indian restaurant in downtown Atlanta. He never would have ventured inside on his own but he wanted his date to be impressed. No matter how out of place he felt in the crowd.

Crystal knew he came from a deeply religious home where no one drank, smoked, or cursed. She was hoping they would fuck because she was horny. But no such luck. After the date, he walked her to the door and gave her a goodnight handshake. This was a part of the saving himself for marriage thing he mentioned. "I would like to see more of you," he said holding her hand but not her gaze.

You could see all of me now, Crystal thought, but just said, "Sure!"

Dave and Crystal went out several times a week, in addition to their daily lunches at work. It had been months and she still got no further than a handshake. Crystal remained drug and alcohol free but she wanted some dick. She craved it. She finally decided that she would get some one way or another. She didn't intend on leaving Dave but if he wouldn't fuck her someone would. Gladly!

Chapter 17

Crystal spent every spare second with her younger sister. She couldn't make up for lost time so she indulged Charity in everything she desired. Movies, skating, mall, whatever she wanted. That even included a rap concert where some young blacks cursed to a heavy drum beat and bass line that moved her insides around. Crystal caught herself deeply inhaling the aroma of the thousand or so joints being smoked.

She felt a slight stirring in her soul, but shook it off. She was clean. The two gorgeous sisters turned heads as the walked Charity's new puppy through their sub division. Even a Rabbi swerved to avoid hitting a parked car, distracted by the two sets of tan legs. A loud racket behind the girls caught both of their attention and they turned to investigate. Crystal frowned at the gaudy custom S.U.V playing music so loud the windows of nearby houses shivered in tune. It was the same song Charity rapped along with word for vulgar word at the concert.

When he pulled up along side of them flashing a diamond-studded smile Charity lost her mind. "Oh my god! Oh my god! It's you!" she screamed hopping up and down pointing at the young black man.

"You know him?" Crystal asked sharing her concerned frown back and forth between them.

"Oh my god yes!" she screamed. "That's Erv-G! Only the best rapper in the whole world!"

Erv-G smiled expansively at the accolades before speaking. "I just moved in 'round the corner. We are shooting a video Saturday. Y'all come through," he said to

Crystal's legs, breasts and ass. Crystal had fucked a few rappers when she worked for Damian but Erv-G she would fuck for free, if not for Dave.

"We will so be there!" Charity exclaimed loudly.

"You a little too young, Shawty," Erv-G said apologetically. "But you are welcome to come."

"No thank you," Crystal politely decline.

"Come on it'll be fun. Besides I'll give you a bunch of autographed merchandise for your lil' sister," Erv-G offered clinching the deal.

"Yesss!" Charity said pumping her little fist as if she had made the winning putt.

"Saturday 1pm. Dress sexy," he said and pulled off.

"You have to go! Please, please, please," Crystal's sister begged.

"Ok, I'll go," she relented and she definitely intended to dress sexy. "Not a word to mom, dad or Dave!"

"Swear to God. I won't say a word!" Charity said checking her sister out in her full-length mirror. Her luscious body was giving the strings of her string bikini all they could handle. Crystal put on a pair of the shorts and a t-shirt to make her exit.

The heels concealed in her bag were the same color red as the bathing suit ensuring all eyes would be on her. She had to park all the way down the street because of all the cars filling the once quiet block. The time on her watch read 2:30 which was right on time for a one o-clock meeting. Crystal was familiar with C.P.T. or colored people time, which meant add an hour and a half.

The party, which doubled as a video shoot, was going full blast when Crystal sashayed into the back yard. Several cameramen swung their cameras at her instantly. Although she wasn't the only white girl in attendance, none could hold a candle to her. Or as a rapper would say, 'they couldn't see her.' She found Erv-G reclining on a lounge chair with an extremely well built, dark girl dancing hard. A cameraman struggled to keep up with her movements as she made her ass checks clap. Crystal walked right into the scene and showed her own moves. Actually they were the ones Jasmine had taught her but she made them her own. People began to flock around to watch the battle. The camera-man had to fight to maintain his position.

The black stallion ran through a battery of sexy moves that Crystal matched gyration for gyration. They competed until the song finally ended as the director yelled "cut".

Erv-G jumped up with an obvious erection in his pants. He grabbed both of the dancers and rushed them inside. Once he got them to his bedroom, Erv-G stripped and dove on the huge bed.

The sense of urgency didn't allow time for Crystal to think. She rushed to get out of her bikini before the black girl. They stripped frantically and race to be first to put the rapper's dick in their mouth. The black girl was a tad quicker and swallowed half the shaft while Crystal kissed his chest. "Y'all share that," Erv-G directed them allowing her access as well.

The orgy lasted well past nightfall, only pausing for the rapper to smoke weed or return texts and emails. Crystal returned home the next morning with all kinds of personalized and autographed memorabilia for her little sister. Of course, she got a little something out of the deal as well. Relief.

Chapter 18

Crystal and Dave were seeing more and more of each other, in the purely figurative sense. On Christmas night, when Dave announced he had something of utmost importance to speak with her about, she just knew he was ready to fuck. She sure was.

Dave was already downstairs chatting with Bob and Mary when Crystal finally finished dressing. "What?" she chuckled apprehensively at the silly grins on everyone's face. All eyes turned to Dave who took a deep breath and dropped to one knee.

Crystal looked at him oddly wondering what he was doing. He didn't have to perform to get some pussy. As long as he performed once he did. "Crystal?" he began, pausing to reach into his pocket. "Will you marry me?"

Is that it! Marry you? You mean you don't wanna fuck me? Crystal's mind screamed but her mouth said, "Yes, of course I'll marry you."

"Welcome to the family!" Bob said proudly and embraced his future son-in-law.

Mary made it a group hug while Crystal pouted. Dave took Crystal out to celebrate and to her surprise pulled up to a popular nightclub.

"You come here?" she asked incredulously.

"No, no," he chuckled "I figured you may like it." He figured right. He was a good sport and stayed on the crowded dance floor until she got tired. They were both hot and sweaty when they finally retreated to a table. Dave motioned for a waitress and caught one's attention. Meanwhile, Crystal viewed one of the huge overhead monitors.

On the screens, the video accompanying whatever song being blasted through the sound system could be viewed and Crystal's heart almost stopped when she saw a familiar ass shaking away on the TV. She breathed a sigh of relief when a waitress came to take their order and kept Dave's eyes off the monitors. "Bring us a couple of iced teas please," he said.

"Make it champagne! We're celebrating," Crystal chimed.

"Crystal No!" Dave yelled startling both women. "We do not drink!"

"What's this we?" she shot back. "I'll drink when I damn well please."

Dave tried to turn away, embarrassed by the outburst, but that would have put a monitor square in front of him, featuring her gyrating her ass in the rapper's face.

"Just take me home!" she demanded rising to her feet. Crystal marched towards the door with Dave on her heels apologizing. Crystal wasn't mad but the ploy worked.

Now she decided to take it a step further and see if she could get fucked out the deal. After riding halfway back to Sugar Hill in silence, Dave tried his luck at apologizing once more. "Look, I'm sorry. I understand I can not dictate to you what you can and can't do," he admitted.

"It's fine Dave. It's just I'm very stressed. I need... I need..."

"What? Name it!" Dave asked eagerly.

"Fuck me" Crystal said plainly "I want, no I need you to fuck my brains out."

Dave was so shocked and embarrassed the car swerved. He was beet red as the word "fuck" was a slap in the face.

"My morals mean nothing to you, do they?" he whispered. "It means nothing to you that I stand for what I believe in. "

"No it doesn't!" she spat back crossing her arms over her chest. She pouted just like she did when she was five. Except now she wanted some dick, not candy.

When Dave pulled into the driveway, Crystal jumped out and slammed the door. Ever the gentleman he still waited until she was safely inside before pulling off.

"What's wrong with you?" Mary inquired at the entrance of her distressed child.

"Nothing," she replied attempting to hit the steps and retreat into her bedroom.

"Wait! Come join me," Mary called out, pouring a glass of the wine she was sipping on.

"Mom, how did you know dad was the one for you?" Crystal asked taking a seat and the glass. "I mean, you guys are so different"

"Yes it may appear we're different. Before I met your father, I dated jocks and bad boys, but when I met him I knew
instantly," Mary explained.

"I feel that way about Dave! I do but...he wont touch me! At all," she admitted.

"Wow, sounds just like your dad," Mary sighed flashing back to the frustration.

"How did you manage?" Crystal asked eagerly.

"Badly. I snuck around and had sex with other guys. I feel horrible about it. I was very immature," Mary offered,
shaking her head.

"So what do I do?" Crystal pleaded.

"Dave's a keeper!" she said plainly.

Crystal apologized to Dave the next day but also put her foot down. She laid out some ground rules that included her hanging out with her friends from time to time. Dave was so happy not to have lost the love of his life that he readily accepted the terms. She probably could have told him she intended to sleep around a little and he would probably have gone for that as well.

Chapter 19

Beth and some of the other girls were home from college and decided to hook up. When they got wind of Crystal's engagement, they insisted upon taking her out to celebrate. The group ended up at the same club Dave took Crystal to the previous week. To her delight, some of the same hot guys she spotted last week were back this week. And why wouldn't they be. A good fisherman returns to the same hole time after time.

All the girls minus Jen, who was tasked with guarding the bags, hit the dance floor. Crystal was a huge hit when the Erv-G video came on. She mimicked what she did on the dance floor while it was on all the displays. When they finally made it back to the table, they ordered end-less champagne and shots. Soon all the girls were tipsy and giggly. Beth went into her purse and unfolded a small package. Using a cut stain she took a quick hit up each nostril.

The package went to Jen, then Darla and finally made its way to Crystal who was trying to reason with herself. It's just a little coke. A few hits will not hurt me she thought as she accepted the drug. Only it wasn't coke and she felt the difference instantly. "What is this!" she exclaimed as euphoria swept through her whole self.

"It's crystal, Crystal," Jen giggled. "Oh my god! Tell me it's not your first time doing meth?"

"It is and it feels so good," Crystal moaned. She could not believe how good she felt. She felt happy, powerful and pretty. She felt super! Then horny. The feelings were mutual and all the girls scanned the packed club in search of prey.

"Pick one for us," Beth whispered in Crystal's ear.

The little squeeze she gave Crystal's thigh explained the rest. "How about him?" Crystal said pointing at a nerdy

Asian guy.

"Too small" Beth shot back.

"What about him?"

"Who? The black guy?" she asked sounding repulsed at the suggestion.

Seeing that her long-time friend had yet acquired a taste for dark meat, Crystal cleaned it up. "No the tall guy behind him," she said pointing to a Jersey shore-ish looking guy.

"That's the one! Let's see if he wants to do sex with us," she giggled and led the way.

"You guys are so bad," Jen laughed as they stalked their prey. She was hoping they all left because she had her eye on the black guy herself. She loved dark meat.

Beth and Crystal approached the man from both sides. They each took an arm and guided him towards the exit.

"Where are we going?" the lucky guy asked with a chuckle.

"To fuck your brains out!" Beth answered.

"Yeah, or suck it out through your cock!" Crystal added.

The man was so happy he left his date at the bar and went to the nearest hotel.

Crystal used meth with at least one of her friends' everyday. It was indeed better than crack, as Kat had told her years back. She could eat, think and function better on meth than with crack. Crack was so time consuming. Once you took a hit you had to follow it up with another, then another and so on, and so on. Not with meth, a couple of lines and away you went. If it had a draw back it was that it made her horny, if that could be considered a draw back. The only problem she had was where to find it once her girlfriends went back to school. Then, she remembered Kat. The woman who answered the phone of the last number Crystal had for Kat seemed annoyed by the mention of her name. "She... does not reside here anymore," she stated plainly.

"Oh I'm sorry. This is the number she gave me at Shady Oaks and..."

"Shady Oaks! Yes, yes that would be in order. One moment. Let me retrieve the address we have on her," the woman said urgently. A moment later, she returned and recited an address in Atlanta.

Kat was living in the eclectic little Five Points neighborhood. It was where you went in Atlanta for all things spiked or mohawked. Tattoo shops and vintage clothing stores lined the streets along with bars and nice restaurants. Crystal stood in front of an old but well-maintained building, checking the numbers on its brick façade. It matched the one on the paper she held. Satisfied that she had the right address, she rang the bell.

"Who is it?" Kat's distinctive voice emanated from the tiny intercom speaker.

"Come out and see for yourself," Crystal demanded changing her voice. "You redheaded stepchild!"

"Crystal? Oh my God. Is that you Crystal Blue?!" Kat screamed upon hearing the pet name. Seconds later, she burst through the door and bear-hugged her old friend on the busy sidewalk. They took the reunion inside Kat's sparsely furnished apartment. Kat looked the same but different with her bright red hair cut into a short pixie style.

A large tattoo covered her entire left arm and featured exotic birds, tribal signs and

Chinese letters along with her multiple piercings. "Wow you look great!" Crystal said once they got settled inside.

"You too! I can't believe you're here! Why are you here?" Kat asked suspiciously.

Crystal thought fast and held up her left hand showing the two carat diamond ring.

"I want all my closest friends in my wedding," she lied, wondering how she would look in a dress.

"Oh my god!" Kat screamed coming over to further inspect the rock. "When? Where? To who!"

Crystal filled her in on Dave and life in general. Of course she left out the bad parts including a second visit to rehab, but Kat left out her subsequent trips back to Shady Oaks as well.

"So I called your house and a lady gave me your address," Crystal said summing it all up. "Yeah, me and the old lady ain't hitting it off too well. Old bitty tried to blame me for everything that came up missing from the house! Kat explained. "So anyway, I'm modeling now. Sexy stuff, DVD's, and magazines."

"Do you know where I can score meth?" Crystal finally blurted out as if she couldn't contain the question a second longer.

"Meth?" Kat laughed. "This is little five points! The street are packed with the stuff!" She grabbed her cordless phone, spoke quickly and hung up. "Three minutes," Kat said exaggerating only slightly. Five minutes later the doorbell rang. When the extremely tattooed man came in, Kat lept into his arms and jammed her tongue down his throat. He was about to drop his pants until Kat pointed at her friend.

"My bad, I didn't see you," he apologized with a laugh. "I'm Two."

"Crystal," she said.

"Oh my favorite," he said attempting to be sexy

. "That's why I called. My friend wants to score," Kat explained.

"Cool, what ya trying to spend," Two asked eagerly.

"Just give me say, two hundred dollars' worth," Crystal said fishing through her purse.

She and the dealer exchanged dope for dollars and Two bid them farewell. But not before giving her a card with a large number Two on it and his cell number underneath. Crystal immediately fixed some lines on the coffee table and inhaled them.

"Have some?" she offered as the drug rushed through her system.

"Um sure, just save me some. I'll shoot it after I eat," Kat said. They chatted for a few more minutes until Crystal lied about a date with Dave.

As soon as the door closed behind her, Kat dissolved the meth and fixed up a needle. After getting it just right she located the tracks under the tattoo and injected herself.

Chapter 20

By the time Dave and Crystals' wedding arrived, she was addicted to meth. She had been snorting the drug almost daily by then. She attempted to stay clean for her big day, but as she dressed she was a mess. Nothing worked and everything upset her.

"I need a minute alone with the bride," Kat announced to Crystal's lifelong friends. No one liked the off little woman with the red hair and no one moved.

"It's ok," Crystal advised sending Beth and Jen reluctantly out of the room.

"Girl you need a hit," Kat whispered. "You're a fucking monster!"

"I know!" Crystal whined. "I tried, I did. I really did. But I need something. Tell me you have something."

"Just a shot I had for later but you can have it," Kat said generously. She pulled a capped syringe filled with a nice unhealthy dose of meth. Crystal turned her head as Kat pulled up her sleeve. She felt a slight pinch from the pin stick and then euphoria.

"You feel it?" Kat asked watching the smile spread on her friend's face.

"Boy, do I!" said Crystal.

When the time came Crystal took her dad's hand and floated down the aisle, grinning from ear to ear. Dave also grinned from ear to ear but for a different reason. Crystal took her place in front of her husband-to-be and exchanged vows. The couple shared their first kiss on command of the preacher. One thing Crystal loved about meth was it lasted a long time. Here it was hours later, all the way in the Grand Bahamas and she was still as high as summer gas prices. It would have taken an ounce of constant crack smoking to achieve this and even then it wouldn't be as good.

"Well Mrs. Atkins, what do you think?" Dave asked holding his new wife in his arms as they stood on the balcony of the honeymoon suite.

"I love it! And you," Crystal exclaimed. She stared at the full moon reflecting on the black ocean. Then she felt an electric current shoot through her eager body when Dave kissed her. It had been over a week since she last had sex and she was beyond ready.

Dave led her back into the room where they slowly disrobed each other.

Yesss! Crystal cheered mentally when she saw Dave was packing. She fought the urge to put the hard, pretty dick in her mouth, knowing it would freak him out. He was as innocent and naïve as a ten-year old. He was genius at everything else but in this realm, he was clueless.

The couple kissed, and fondled until finally he pushed deep inside of her. It was the first time either of them made love in their lives. The honeymoon was scheduled to last a week but by day three the burning in Dave penis was unbearable. It hurt so badly when he urinated he tried to abstain from drinking. A thick yellowish green discharge forced them to find a local clinic to get treated. A culture swab confirmed that they both had gonorrhea.

"How could that be? We haven't had sex before! This is our honeymoon for goodness sakes!" Dave whined upon hearing the diagnosis.

"Well, it very common disease," the Bahamian lady doctor said matter-of-factly.

"Not for us! We're both virgins! Well, we were," Dave exclaimed causing the woman to cast a suspicious glance at Crystal.

"I must have gotten it from using a dirty towel," she urged. "Um... at the um...gym.

"A towel?" Dave frowned. "Is that possible?"

The doctor looked at Crystal who begged her without a word to agree. "I've lived long enough to know that anything is possible," she said honestly.

When the doctor produced the syringes to shoot the couple with penicillin, Crystal's mouth instantly watered. She craved Meth like her life depended upon it.

"Let's just go home," she announced sadly once they returned to the room.

"It's not your fault," Dave comforted, but it was to no avail. Crystal was ready to go home.

Three days with no meth was enough.

Chapter 21

"Oh my god! You did not burn your husband! On your honeymoon!" Kat exclaimed when she was told the story.

"I did, I did and I know exactly where I got it from," Crystal said reflecting back to a recent one-night stand. She let some guy talk her into a quickie outside of a club.

A few lines of meth and a couple of martinis later and Crystal was bent over a car in the back alley.

She fumed. "Bastard, couldn't even make me cum! I had to go home and finish myself off."

"Ready?" Kat sang holding a filled syringe. Crystal held out her arm and watched as her friend injected the drug into her veins.

"Mmm thanks," Crystal moaned. She gathered her belongings and headed to class. At her husband's suggestion she had re-enrolled in school. The goal was to finish what she had started. She was a student by day and a devoted housewife at night. A quick fix from Kat each morning and Crystal was off and running.

The Atkins home life was ideal. They opted to live in Dave's small apartment over use of his granddad's upscale condo. Bob put his son-in-law on salary, most of which went towards savings for their first home. This was where Crystal got her dope though.

The drugs still made Crystal horny and Dave did not disappoint. After missing all that good high school and college pussy, Dave could not get enough. Crystal had trained him how to please her and he did, daily. Life was good, for a while. Then in an instant, the downward spiral began.

One day Crystal was walking across campus basking in the warm glow of the meth shot she had earlier when her name was called. The voice was familiar and she scanned her surroundings looking for its owner.

84

"Crystal, is that you?" Keisha approached wearing a humorless smile. "It is you!"

"Well I don't have time to talk," Crystal said curtly and turned to walk off.

"I can't believe you have the audacity to show your face around here after what you did to my brother," Keisha called after her. She immediately called her newly released brother Damian, who called the newly released Black.

The two vengeful men raced downtown and scouted the campus in vain for their prey. They staked out the school for weeks wasting their time. Crystal would not be returning.

Now her days were spent in Kat's apartment. At least she was continuing her education by learning to cook her own shots and injecting herself. Higher learning if you will.

Her nights were spent satisfying her near insatiable appetite for sex. As a result, she was pregnant soon after. Dave was absolutely thrilled at the thought of becoming a parent. Crystal, not so much. Her primary concern was how this would affect her drug life.

It didn't. Everyday she fixed up a batch and shot up. Even as her belly grew, she continued to use. She used the household ATM card so much the name wore off of it.

Crystal felt her first contraction shortly after Dave departed for the office. Knowing she would be stuck in the hospital for at least the rest of the day, she fixed up a dose to get her through. "It's time," she informed Dave via text message. Minutes later, he barged into the apartment in a panic telling Crystal not to panic. He called their doctor en route to the hospital and told him to rush down.

Crystal was admitted into her private suite to deliver. When her doctor arrived shortly after ,he quickly examined her.

"Well," he said with a hand in her vagina. "You're not fully dilated yet. We'll have to wait. Shouldn't be long." But it was long. Some eight hours later and still no baby.

Bob and Mary were waiting along with Dave's parents. The doctor was back and forth on the hour, only to announce that she still wasn't ready.

By the next morning, Crystal was in agony. Not just from the impending labor but she desperately wanted a shot of meth. She actually contemplated calling Kat and having her rush a dose over. Dave did the best he could to comfort her by shoveling ice chips onto her parched mouth. The doctor finally announced she was fully dilated and began delivery.

Crystal had her feet firmly in the stirrups, pushing as commanded by the doctor. Her motivation was the long-awaited hit she had coming once the baby was out of her.

"Wow!" Dave exclaimed in wonderment as his son's head emerged from Crystal's womb. A few more pushes and he made his entrance into the world.

The doctor and nurses shared a shocked look, alarming the new parents. The umbilical cord was cut and the child was whisked away before they got a chance to hold him. Before they could even hear him cry as newborns do.

"There seems to be some complications," the doctor said stitching her back up.

"What's wrong with our child?" Dave asked anxiously

"We're not sure. We'll run a few tests and let you know," he said wrapping up.

As soon as Crystal was stitched up, the doctor rushed to check on the newborn. Both sets of grandparents came into the room to await news on the baby's condition.

"He'll be fine," Mary offered attempting to comfort her daughter.

"Yeah the first ones are always the hardest," Dave's mother added.

"Excuse me. We need a little blood," a young pretty nurse sang as she entered the room. Crystal offered her arm causing the smile to dissipate from the nurse face.

She frowned at the obvious tracks marks as she tapped into a well
-used vein. The needle stick on it further reminded Crystal of how badly she wanted a hit. Another hour had passed before a grim-faced nurse
asked to see the child's father.

"We'll come too," Dave's mom insisted.

"Us too," Bob added rising from his seat.

They all followed the nurse up one floor to the doctor's nondescript
office. "Have a seat," he offered solemnly. The doctor frowned as he
double-checked the file. He took a deep breath delivering the bad news.
"Mr. Atkins, how long has your wife been using methamphetamines?"
he asked bluntly.

"Using what?" Dave frowned confused at the question. "My wife
does not use drugs."

Bob and Mary shared a glance and lowered their heads.

"Yes sir, she does, according to the blood test we just gave her quite
recently," the doctor shot back.

"The baby! What's wrong with the baby?" Mrs. Atkins pleaded.

The baby has been affected by heavy pre-natal drug use." The doctor
gave them a few seconds to digest the statement before continuing.
"I'm afraid he is severely brain damaged, blind and un-able to breath on
his own," he laid out.

"Will he get better? Grow out of it?" Mary desperately asked.

"No, he won't. He will not survive. I'm sorry."

The sad news shocked the father and grandparents. The silence
broke down into subdued sobs. They helplessly threw out futile treatment options before accepting little David's fate. He was a dead baby
crawling. At long last,

they all went to speak with Crystal. The decision was made not to
be harsh. Instead they would comfort and encourage. When they tentatively entered the room, it was empty. Crystal was gone!

Chapter 22

Crystal arrived by cab to Kat's apartment and practically crawled to the door. Two had just finished inside of Kat when they heard a slight knock followed by someone moan. Kat threw on a shirt and pulled open the front door. There was Crystal seated, leant against the wall. Behind her was an irate taxi driver demanding to be paid.

"Oh my God, Cryssy! Are you ok?" Kat asked helping her friend to her feet.

"No, I need a fix," she moaned. "I just escaped from the hospital moments after delivering a child deformed by my bad choices."

"I know you do baby," Kat comforted before directing Two to go pay the driver.

She fixed a needle for her and quickly ran it into her arm.

"Ahhh," Crystal sighed as the drugs cruised through her body. Over the next few weeks, Kat nursed Crystal back to...health. That entailed lots of fast food, sodas and meth. Herbal therapy largely amounted to a lot of marijuana. Kat had received her trust fund a few months prior and was rushing through it as quickly as she possibly could. It was as if her intention was to go back to being broke as soon as possible.

Once Crystal was up and running, it was time to party. Kat treated her to a shopping spree. She opted for a new sexy look to go with her new life. She would not be going home.

Each day began with a shot of meth, weed and eventually lines of coke. At night, they hit the clubs and partied into the wee hours. Most nights, they left with a couple of guys to have their way with. Sometimes, only one guy. Six months later when Kat's well ran dry, the party train came to an abrupt halt. That left the two women with raging drug habits that needed constant and immediate attention. Luckily Crystal knew where she could get some money.

"May I speak with Mr. Atkins please?" Kat said in her most professional voice as

Dave's receptionist came on the line.

"He is on his other line. Would you care to hold, or can I take a message?" the equally professional woman replied managing to smile through the phone.

"No I'll call back," Kat said. She thanked her and hung up. "He's there! Let's do this!"

This was breaking into Crystal's old apartment in search of cash and valuables. To both of their surprise, Crystal's key easily opened the door granting her access to the world she left behind.

To Crystal's lone surprise all her belongings were exactly how she left them. Dave hoped and prayed she would come back one day, so he left her stuff intact. I guess this is where the old adage of being careful what you wish for applies, because Crystal was back, but she was stuffing her pockets with valuables. She decided to spare Dave and leave his jewelry in the box. It didn't matter because Kat stole it as soon as Crystal turned her head. Crystal loaded some of the clothes she missed most into a bag. She swiped a bankcard linked to the substantial savings account along with a laptop before leaving and locking the door. The first stop was the mall where Crystal returned Kat's shopping spree. The women spent thousands of dollars on clothes and trinkets. She also withdrew the fifteen hundred dollars daily limit to use in the club. Two got five hundred of the money for meth, while the coke guy got another five. After the weed man got his cut, the money was almost gone. Crystal charged eight hundred more on cab rides and bars as they partied the night away. When the sun rose the next morning all the money was gone. When she tried the ATM card the following afternoon, the machine promptly ate it. They tried their luck again at the apartment but the locks had been changed and fortified.

Undaunted, they found a pawnshop who took all of Crystal's jewelry off her hands for a thousand dollars. Being a lot more frugal with the money, it lasted three days before the girls were broke again.

"No worries, I'll call my agent in the a.m." Kat suggested. "He'll have some work for us."

"Sure," Crystal agreed. Anything to keep the party going. Kats agent was actually a low budget porn director. The only modeling she had done was with a cock in her mouth. When Rocco got a gander at beautiful Crystal, he immediately offered her a thousand dollars for the day.

Kat bitched about never being paid more than five for any given day and got a raise.

Crystal usually got horny when she got high so getting paid to get laid was a win/win for her. The girls had spent the last of their money on their daily hit so they needed the income. They met at an upscale hotel that would serve as the set. Crystal was already damp from the anticipation of sex. Rocco and his camera man where already at the room when the girls arrived. They quickly dressed or better yet undressed into the skimpy outfits from the wardrobe bag.

When Rocco answered the knock on the room door, two tall black men walked in and Kat lost her mind. "I will not let some nappy-headed nigger touch me!" she demanded.

The men frowned and looked at Rocco for an explanation.

"Easy guys. No problem here. We will work it out," he said quickly. The two were big stars in the industry and it was a feather in his cap to have gotten them.

"I'll do it!" Crystal exclaimed eagerly. She had slept with several black men by then and had no qualms about doing it again. Besides, they needed the money.

"Great!" Rocco cheered. That would be more to his liking anyway. Having the two black stallion's pummel a pretty blonde was the stuff of porn legends.

"Tell me you're not going to do this," Kat pleaded. She was repulsed at the thought of any one other that her own race.

"What choice do we have?" Crystal replied and headed over to the bed. The script, if you could call it that, called for her to be laid across the bed reading, when all of a sudden two naked black men walk in. Only in porn. After a few lines of corny porn dialog to accompany the cheesy porn music, Crystal took the first man deep in her throat. The man's knees buckled when his dick touched her tonsils.

The other man came around and arranged her so he could lap his huge tongue on her vagina. Kat regretted her racism when the expert licked Crystal to a violent orgasm. The first man was now fully erect and slid into the quivering vagina as the other took his place in her mouth.

"I'll give you an extra five hundred bucks if you jump in there," Rocco said to Kat sweetening the deal. No sooner did the words clear his mouth did Crystal come again, making the deal that much sweeter.

"You want fuck me nigger?" Kat spat venomously as she climbed onto the bed and into the scene. The black man in Crystals' mouth looked at her oddly as she lay back and spread her legs. He was confused and shot a glance over to Rocco who motioned him on. The large man aimed his huge dick at Kat's pussy and rammed himself inside.

"Arrgh!!" Kat exclaimed when he hit her cervix. "Fuck this pussy, you black motherfucker!"

Only it wasn't pussy the man was after. He slammed into her viciously in search of a kidney or spleen to rupture. They both hated that it felt so good. Kat continued hurling insults and racial epithets at him causing him to fuck her harder, which was just what she wanted.

"Take this dick you white bitch whore! Piece of shit!" he grunted while pounding.

"You trying to make me cum Kunta Kinte? Huh, Leroy?" Kat yelled both fighting against and longing for the imminent orgasm building. "Ok, ok, you win! I'll cum," she whined as she convulsed.

The actor couldn't take any more and pulled out spaying semen on Kat's body.

"That was fucking great!" Rocco laughed. He loved it and couldn't believe his luck.

This was sure to go down in interracial porn history. Crystal allowed her suitor to ejaculate all over her face and hair, winding up the scene. They scheduled another shoot for the following weekend. Kat made sure to slide Kunta Kinte her cell number.

Chapter 23

The girls partied hard with their new source of income until the feds came knocking. Rocco was arrested and indicted on charges from Atlanta to his native Brooklyn. The well had officially run dry.

"A buddy of mine owns the Hall. I can get you guys in. Especially you, Crystal,"

Two said as he ran a shot of meth into Kats foot. "What's that supposed to mean? Especially her!" Kat demanded.

"I'm just saying, um you know guys like dumb blondes." Two laughed, attempting to clean up the statement. The Hall was a seedy step club located on Bedford Highway and it catered to a mixed crowd. The club featured Black, White and Latino dancers.

Crystal readily accepted, sucked in by the lure of easy cash daily. The party must go on. She had been in Damian's club plenty of times but since she was regulated to turning trips in the back rooms, she had never hit the stage. Nonetheless, she had learned a variety of dance moves from her time spent with Jasmine.

On the girls' first night, they floated in high off fresh shots. Kat was first to hit the stage and received a lukewarm reception. She was as pretty enough but her small frame was out of place in a strip club. A few men watched and offered dollar bills but the majority of the patrons were not enthused. Most carried on private conversations waiting for another dancer to take the pole position.

When Crystal arrived on the stage the club took notice. The pretty blue-eyed blonde was a breath of fresh air compared to her trailer-trash counterpart. Then she moved like the black girls. The men rushed the stage handing tips of tens and twenties vying for her attention. It was literally raining money as Crystal shook her ass to the music.

At the end of the night, Crystal left with slightly over a grand to Kat's two hundred. The relationship between the two changed in an instant. Kat became curt and downright nasty towards her from that night on. Crystal couldn't figure out what happened until she overheard Kat talking about her to Two. The malicious lies held one truth, it was time to move.

The first move was to an extended stay motel. A stone's throw from the club, the small room was jammed packed with clothes and personal effects. The one hundred fifty dollars a week rent left her plenty of money for more important things, drugs. A few nights a week, Crystal would select a customer to go home with. Sometimes she went to the highest bidder sometimes the one most likely to please her. Soon she had built a fan base of regulars who assisted in various aspects of life. Mr. Pits managed an upscale apartment complex. Crystal fucked her way into a nice one bedroom unit. Mr. Hodges supplied all the furnishings from his store in exchange for his weekly visits.

A cocaine dealer named Arnell had taken a liking to Crystal's throat and dropped off an eight ball or more for a blowjob. She had a good run. A great one, in fact, but no one can use that much drugs and not be adversely affected. They were slowly wearing her down.

To make matters worse, Darnell accidently left an eight ball of crack cocaine instead of the powered variety. Crystal ignored it for a couple of days until 'it' finally convinced her to smoke it. That first hit was the first of thousands to come. As if adding insult to injury, or kicking someone when they're down, Crystal added another addictive drug into her life. She still shot meth for breakfast, then smoked crack periodically throughout the day.

At first, Darnell had refused to sell her any more dope. He knew the ramifications of its use, but ultimately he was a drug dealer and money was god. He fucked the daylights out of her one last time before she officially became a customer. Crystal's routine changed overnight as crack became a habit. She began blowing customers off in favor of sucking a pipe. As a result her weight began to plummet causing her to lose even more of her regulars. Mr. Pitt asked her to move out of the apartment in favor of someone younger, cleaner and more coherent. Back in the motel, she decided to try her hand back in the Hall. She was almost tossed out once the manager got a look at her. Crystal was still as pretty as ever but her frame was rail thin. He felt bad enough to give here one last shot. When the name 'Crystal Blue' was announced as next on stage a wave of excitement swept through the club. It instantly turned into shocked horror as the shell

of the former beauty took the stage.

"Is that the same one?" a confused patron asked.

"Looks like her mom maybe," came one reply.

"Grand mom is more like it," came another.

She looked so pitiful on the stage. A few men offered sympathy tips while most averted their eyes. Finally, the owner gave her a hundred dollars from his own pocket and asked her to leave. Leave she did with one hundred fourteen dollars.

After securing her meth. Crystal called Darnell to spend the remaining fifty but he refused to meet her for that paltry sum. "Betta take yo ass down to Fulton Industrial. You might be able to turn a trick or two and get some money to spend," he said harshly before hanging up on her.

Fulton Industrial Blvd. was an industrial area of west Atlanta known for truckers and prostitutes. With those two vital elements in place, a flourishing drug market was a given. Crystal turned right after exiting I-20 and immediately saw the tall tale signs of drug activity. Young black men moved about running up to cars to supply their wares.

She pulled into the parking lot for a particularly busy motel and parked. She chose to park on the side opposite the dealers and walk over. As she made her way over she spied several cars whose drivers were leaned back enjoying a blowjob. Darnell's statement of turning a few tricks popped into her head. It would have been a smart move to suck a dick or two while she was there, but she was too eager to get high. She exchanged the last fifty bucks she had for five small clear bags containing five small rocks. After driving a half an hour she drove back over and turned a few tricks in the parking lot.

She was shocked to learn that a blowjob only fetched twenty bucks on the street. It took five of them to get enough money for enough drugs to get her through the night. The next morning Crystal ran a shot of meth in her foot to start the day. She forced herself to eat a burger knowing that once she started smoking she would not stop to eat.

When Crystal arrived to Fulton Industrial during the day she was amazed at how dramatically the climate had changed. It was now a busy, bustling thoroughfare. Instead of the Black and Latino Johns she serviced the night before, the strip now had white professional types cruising for action.

There was also a lot more competition. On every corner she saw scantily clad whores for sale. Crystal parked in the motel from the previous night to set up shop. She only walked three feet before a middle-aged white man pulled to a stop. He hit the unlock button on his spanking new Volvo and invited her in.

"Date?" he smiled waving a fifty-dollar bill. Ten minutes later she exited the vehicle fifty dollars richer. This immediately repeated itself and then repeated once more.

"Hey don't be taking all my business!" a squeaky voice called behind Crystal as she hopped out of her fourth car. Fear swept through Crystal thinking she may have been intruding on someone's turf. She whipped around prepared to apologize or run and saw a tiny black woman smiling back at her.

"I'm sorry I'm new... I just..." Crystal stammered.

"Just messing with you girl," she laughed as she approached. "I aint like these other hoes out here trying claim no spot. My name's Annette but err body call me 'Lil Bit.'"

"Well hey Lil' Bit. My name is Crystal." She was relieved not to have trouble.

"You new around here? I aint seent you round hur?" Lil bit announced. "You smoke?"

"Do I!" Crystal exclaimed eagerly.

The two fast friends retreated to Lil' Bit's room and shared a few hits. The buddies turned a few more tricks and went back to smoke some more. By the end of the day, Crystal drove over to collect her belongings from her hotel and moved in with Lil' Bit.

Crystal still shot her meth in the morning but the rest of the day was spent tricking for crack. Customers wanted head, which left her longing for cock. She would occasionally go out at night in search of some black john generous with his money and dick. They didn't mind paying for the still pretty white girl. It was a win/win situation in the streets.

One night after returning from one such episode, she found the room empty. It struck her as off since Lil' Bit rarely ventured out at night. Crystal began smoking lightly trying to save some for her buddy. She tried but failed. Lil' Bit still hadn't returned by the next morning. This troubled Crystal but it didn't stop the show. She shot up and rushed out to catch the noon rush. The nearby executives loved a stiff drink and blowjob for lunch.

Today was particularly busy and Crystal was turning tricks left and right, in and out of cars at a fast pace. Just as she exited one car, she spied the coveted red truck. All the whores on patrol knew that its driver spent handsomely for a few minutes of work. It was rounding the corner where several other prostitutes sold themselves. Crystal knew she had to act fast so she took off after it.

She ducked trough a wooded area in attempt to cut him off. As she ran she tripped over something, falling flat on her face.

"Shit!!!" Crystal cursed, pounding her first on the earth. The red truck pulled to a stop allowing a crack whore inside. She looked to see what tripped her and cost her a hundred dollar john. It was a leg. Lil Bit's dead leg attached to her dead body.

Chapter 24

The murder of her friend barely caused a ripple in the fabric of life along Fulton Industrial. Lil' Bit was stuffed inside a child-sized body bag with the scarf used to choke her still attached to her neck. Authorities were in and out in under a half hour. A cat stuck in a tree in her old neighborhood would have gotten more attention.

"I gotta go home," Crystal announced to no one in particular. It had finally dawned on her just how far away from home she really was. "After today, this is it!" she declared firmly.

"Date ma'am?" a handsome cowboy type asked politely, pulling Crystal back to the task at hand. Tricking. "Sure!" Crystal beamed, pre-paid to climb aboard the mini monster truck.

"Do you have a room? I reckon I would like to fuck," he announced in a twang that could only be grown in Texas.

"I reckon I do," said Crystal. She had been sucking old dicks all day, so a good fucking would be a welcome change.

Since Crystal didn't wear much clothing, she was naked in a flash. She sat on the bed and eagerly watched the cowboy undress. She gave him enough head to get him fully erect and laid back. He rolled a condom down his shaft and went to work. He gave her a thorough fucking that was both firm yet tender. Crystal pretended he was her boyfriend. And they were making love for the first time. The illusion worked and she came just before he did.

"Thank you, kindly ma'am," the cowboy announced as he put his clothes back on. He was so polite he probably would have tipped his hat had he had it on.

"No thank you!" Crystal smiled still buzzing from the good sex. She opened her purse to add his money to hers allowing him to see her bankroll. It was only a couple of hundred dollars but to a crack-addicted cowboy on the run, it was a gold mine.

"Close ya eyes little lady. I have a surprise for ya," he smiled placing one hand behind his back.

"A surprise!" Crystal gushed and quickly complied.

"No peeking," He lifted her chin up. She closed her eyes tightly and never saw the blow coming. Since he had actually been a cowpuncher, the girl didn't stand a chance.

The blow knocked her out cold. He quickly removed the money from her purse then rummaged around the room in search of valuables, finding none. This time he did tip his hat as he left the room. "Ma'am," he nodded as he closed the door behind him.

Crystal wasn't going to feel so lucky when she finally awoke but John Wayne Merick had killed four prostitutes in as many states. She was very lucky indeed. The blow allowed Crystal to get some much needed sleep. It was well after dark when she finally awoke. It still took several minutes to piece together the events leading to the empty purse and huge lump on her head. Nevertheless, the show had to go on. There was meth to be shot and crack to be smoked. That meant that some dicks had to be sucked.

As Crystal made her way down to the street, she passed a room full of boys she knew to be sellers. She knew better than to ask for credit, but these were extenuating circumstances, to her anyway. "Excuse me, but I'm... well, will you front me a dime till I can go make me some change," she asked pleadingly.

"Make some change?" one young boy frowned. "What you finna do? Suck some dick?"

"As a matter of fact I am," Crystal shot back. She was far beyond shame at this point of her young life.

"Shit come on to our room, you can hook us up," the other boy announced.

Crystal agreed and followed the two boys to a room containing at least ten more.

Crystal multiplied that dime times ten and thought she had struck gold. Hell, she could blow the room and be smoking in no time.

The young boys ravaged Crystal. She had one in both sides of her at all times. They took turns in her mouth and vagina multiple times. This went on for hours as some left and a couple new ones took their place. She was battered and bruised by the time the last young man came on her. Sticky from semen and beer, Crystal pulled her clothes on as the boys piled out.

"It's on the dresser," the last one said as he left the room.

"Thanks," Crystal said half-heartedly through her sore jaws. She stood up to collect her pay and found one dime-sized rock.

Crystal burst into tears at the sight. She was still crying when she got to her room. She put the entire rock on her pipe and hit it in an attempt to put herself out of her misery. Her heart didn't stop, but she was as high as bubble. All it did was make her crave more. A quick rinse in the shower to remove what the boys left behind and she was back on the block.

As soon as she walked to the street, a late model BMW pulled to a stop beside her but she knew him too well. Crystal didn't know what to say so she just waited. The driver took a deep breath and handed over a hundred dollar bill. Still she didn't know what to do, until he leaned back and pulled out his erect cock. Crystal looked at the man who still refused to even glance in her direction. She shrugged her shoulders and dropped her head into his lap.

It only took a couple of minutes of her expert headman ship before the man grunted and filled her mouth with his cum. As soon as his penis pumped the last spurts of semen, he hit the locks again. It was "john" speak for 'beat it'. Crystal took the hint and got out. She spit her father's semen on the sidewalk as he pulled off. This was as low as she could go. She decided this would be her last night getting high. Her last night on earth.

Bob felt his usual remorse as he drove home. It wasn't the first time he sought a quick blowjob after working late. Knowing Mary would be asleep, he figured the whores where doing both of them a favor. Still he never could bring himself to look or speak to the girl. He did watch this one spit a mouthful of cum from his rearview. It amazed him how much she reminded him of his long lost daughter.

Crystal decided to turn one or two more tricks before heading in. She wanted to ensure she had enough to smoke the night away, and then for an overdose in the morning. Celebrating her last night with no time for the usual formalities and precautions, Crystal jumped into the first car that pulled up. "I'll suck your dick for forty bucks!" she blurted out.

The uniformed officer couldn't believe his luck. For the first time in his tenure a prostitute ran to him instead of away. She was arrested on the spot, charged with prostitution, and thrown in a tank along with the other crack hoes. Since there had long been a missing persons report on her, Crystal's parents were notified of her arrest. Bob and Mary were present for her first court appearance the next morning. Their eyes past over her several times as they scanned the room in search of her.

"Oh my God! Bob, that's her!" Mary said frantically as he recognized her too, from last night. His daughter was the crack whore he had bought.

Mary couldn't take it and rushed from the court room. He couldn't take it either but he stayed. In the end, he was able to pull some strings and get his daughter into an intense rehabilitation center instead of jail. Crystal was going to get some help.

Chapter 25

The Atlanta treatment center was more like a prison than the comfy confines of Shady Oaks. The women were dragged through an intake process designed to degrade them. They were stripped naked and sprayed with a douching solution and then herded into a large open shower. The large mirrors were everywhere to show them just how far they had fallen. Most didn't recognize themselves.

"Crystal?!" said an almost familiar voice from behind.

Crystal scanned her memory for a face. She was almost afraid to turn around since anyone who knew her in here had to be as bad off as she was. "That is you!" A war torn version of her friend and part-time sex partner Jasmine sang.

"Hey girl" Crystal said far more cheerful than she felt. The last thing she wanted or needed was a reminder of her past. The two naked women hugged each other getting only passing glances from the thirty other women on the shower. They had done too many despicable things in their own recent histories to judge. After getting settled, in the girls met up and caught up. Each had horror stories that include Damian somewhere along the way.

"Girl, I'll never forget the way he looked at me when he got arrested," Crystal said shivering at the memory. "He gave me the evilest smile I ever saw in my life."

"Chile don't even worry bout him," said with her sassy 'ghetto girl' head movements. "I stole nine whole ounces from him. He say he gone kill me too."

Jasmine made an advance that caused Crystal to finally end their friendship. Jasmine didn't take rejection well and her drug-induced mental illness only made it worse. In her mind, Crystal was now her enemy and she knew just how to get back at her. Prior to release, all the residents are given an eight hour pass. They would be tested for every known substance upon return to see if the rehab had in fact rehabilitated them.

Jasmine had begged and badgered Crystal so insistently to allow her to treat her to dinner. Crystal finally relented. "Just dinner! No drinks! No sex!" she reiterated, clearly establishing the boundaries. Crystal was moving across the country to Arizona upon release. She had an apartment and was enrolled in school. It would be a new chance at life. The old friends laughed over dinner sharing plans for their new lives. They ate at a nice steakhouse down town, gorging on seafood as well. Jasmine removed a vile from her purse. She dumped a white powdery substance into Crystal's sweet tea and gave it a quick stir.

"Whew!" Crystal sighed as she rejoined her friend.

"My turn, girl," Jasmine said lifting her glass to her girl for a toast. "To a new life." The girls clinked glasses and they downed their tea.

Jasmine went to relieve herself and sent the prearranged code. By the time she returned, Crystal was already woozy from the drug.

"Are you ok," Jasmine asked amazed at how fast the drug worked.

"No I'm....I'm...not," Crystal managed to say. She was seeing double and felt herself slowing down.

"Is everything ok?" a concerned waiter asked seeing the obvious distress.

"Yeah, she's fine. I'll walk her outside," Jasmine said putting money on the table to cover the bill. She helped Crystal out of the restaurant and into the back seat of a waiting car. Jasmine closed the door and walked around to the open driver's window.

"So now we even?" she asked eagerly.

"We straight," Damian replied looking at his prey in the back seat.

"This gonna be fun!" Black announced from the passenger seat. He reached back and fondled Crystal as they pulled off.

When Crystal came to, she was naked and tied to a bed in a cheap motel. The duct tape on her mouth prevented her from screaming at the sight of the two men staring down at her.

"Look who is up?" Damian said cheerfully.

"Time to pay the piper," Black laughed. He reached down and shoved a large finger inside of her.

"Stick to the script," Damian warned as he fixed a syringe. Crystal moaned and pleaded with her eyes, and began to cry.

"Uh uh, don't cry now," Damian spat. "Yo ass ain't cry when you sent me up the river!" She shook her head furiously as he approached with the needle as Black undressed. Her muffled cries intensified as he searched for a vein.

Through the gag, she was trying to say "No I'm clean! I don't want any drugs! Or sex! I'm clean!" But Damian found what he was looking for and injected her. Instantly her whole being became numb and she stopped struggling.

Black had stroked himself to a huge erection that made Damian do a double take. He spit in his hand and used it as lubricant before climbing between Crystal's thighs. Crystal's head fell to the side and she locked eyes with Damian as Black pushed inside of her. She didn't feel a thing even as Black ripped her to shreds, due to the massive dose of heroin coursing through her body. She and Damian maintained eye contact as Black pounded her and her lungs filled with fluid from the overdose. Damian saw the exact moment when she 'let go.' A single tear escaped her eye as he turned to leave. No way was he gonna watch Black fuck a dead body.

The End

The Beginning

Charity was absolutely stunning by age 18. Bob and Mary were extremely overprotective of her and rarely let her out of their sight. After losing Crystal to the world, they would not fail again. Charity knew her infant nephew's ashes were contained in the pretty vase over the mantle. When a teary-eyed Mary added a second vase she knew her long lost sister was inside. It was the same blue as Crystal's eyes, but no one talked about it.

When prom night reared its ugly head, Bob and Mary knew it was time to loosen the grip, a little. Charity's prom date was the mega handsome, mega popular Conner Stephens. The two had been unofficially going steady for months.

Tonight, they planned to make it official. The plan was to make a brief appearance at the prom and then retreat to the reserved suite upstairs, where they could finally spend some time alone. Bob and Mary were impressed with Conner when he arrived at their home. He was indeed charming and had impeccable manners. He presented Mary with a bouquet of flowers that matched the elaborate corsage he bought for Charity. Bob eyed him suspiciously as he pinned it on his daughter's ample chest.

Mary snapped just short of a hundred pictures while Bob manned a video camera. The young couple finally managed to extricate themselves from the house and into the waiting limo.

"There goes our baby," Mary sighed as the limo pulled from the curb.

"Yes, but she'll be back," Bob said confidently.

The limo made one more stop en route to the prom. They picked up Jason and his date Angel, the couple who went half on the two bedroom suite they rented. The foursome made their grand appearance, danced and socialized before heading up to their suite. As requested, a bottle of champagne was waiting on ice. Charity was the only one who had yet to have a drink, but readily accepted a flute. In fact she was a virgin in all regards.

"Let's get this party started!" Jason announced dumping a small pile of white powder on the table.

"Cool!" Angel gushed enthusiastically, scooting to the edge of the seat.

"What's that?" Charity asked confused by its presence and their re-action to its presence. Even Conner was delighted when it made its appearance.

"A little meth!" Jason said while dividing it into four equal lines, one for each person.

"Me first!" Angel sang and leaned forward, using a rolled up bill. She quickly inhaled one of the lines. "Oh my!" she chuckled and leaned back. Conner dove in next and made a line disappeared up his nostril. Next Jason followed suit, leaving only one line left.

"Go on babe. It's great!" Conner urged.

"The best!" Angel cosigned as Jason handed her the bill.

Curiosity and peer pressure pushed Charity's head down and she inhaled the drug. Moments later, a smile

spread on her face as its effects began to be felt.

"A toast!" Conner announced grabbing his glass. Everyone lifted their flutes and clinked them together as Conner made the toast. "To a new beginning!